Emma the Matchmaker

AN AUSTEN INSPIRED ROMANTIC COMEDY

Austen Book 2

Rachel John

ISBN: 9781095694237

ACKNOWLEDGMENTS

This one is for all the Mr. Knightley fans, though I have to admit, I'm still a little partial to Mr. Darcy myself.

I'm so thankful for a supportive husband. I'd also like to thank my proofreader, Lisa Bjornberg, my critique partners Krista Noorman, Franky A. Brown, Melanie Snitker, Anneka Walker, and Danielle Arie. Big thanks to my beta readers, Dawn Malone, Julie Spencer, Anita Heath, Susanne Meyers, and Randi Rigby.

CHAPTER 1 ♥ INTROVERTS UNITE

Short girls do not catch bridal bouquets. Well, not without a lot of effort, and Emma was already hindered by her stiff, lavender bridesmaid dress and her reluctance to participate at all. However, she dutifully stood with the group of giggling single women and waited. The use of the word 'single' being loosely applied here. Some of these girls hadn't left middle school.

This was the worst part of a wedding reception. Okay, this, and when the bride and groom shoved cake into each other's faces like cage fighters. Thankfully, Taylor and West were way too practical for that.

"Ready, girls?" Taylor shouted as she stood with her back to them.

So ready. Emma glanced around and caught George Knightley laughing at her. She shook her head at him and mouthed 'you're next.' The garter toss would have him up here looking like an idiot in a minute. Emma turned back to the gaggle of girls just in time to see the bouquet sail into the hands of one of Taylor's tall cousins. She'd knocked the girls in front of her out of the way to get to it. Classy.

Emma passed George on her way to her seat and gave him a friendly nudge. "Go represent, old man."

He often liked to point out how much older and wiser he was, so it was Emma's duty to remind him he was about to turn thirty. Not that it mattered. The guy got better looking with every passing year. He had that golden-haired, golden-tanned, beach-boy look that turned many a girl's head.

She hurried to Granddad, hoping to distract him from the striptease music for the garter toss blaring out of the speakers. It wasn't so much that Granddad was a prude, but he hadn't yet accepted that his Nurse Taylor was leaving him to go make a life with someone else.

"How is the chocolate pie?" Emma asked, maneuvering her chair to block the dance floor.

Granddad poked at his slice. "Good. I think I'll just have one more bite or it will give me indigestion."

Emma kept him talking, only glancing back once or twice to catch George's red face during the garter toss. He had his hands in his pockets, glancing around as if he'd somehow stumbled on the scene by mistake. Not a lot flustered the guy, so it was fun to see.

As soon as the dancing started up, Emma coaxed Granddad out to the ballroom floor for a spin. "The Way You Look Tonight" was a song just his speed. He shuffled back and forth in his carefully shined shoes, his hand warm and papery against hers.

"The wedding turned out nice. Don't you think?" she asked.

Granddad nodded, humming along to Frank Sinatra. He was so short she could look over his head and see her sister and brother-in-law dancing, her sister's pregnant belly adorably sandwiched between them. They waved, and she waved back.

Frank Sinatra finished his crooning, and a Beatles song came on next. Granddad continued their dance, but he was beginning to slow. He'd been a good sport. An all-day wedding took a lot out of a person, especially someone about to turn ninety.

"Had about all the fun you can stand?" Emma asked.

"I'm afraid if it gets any darker out, you won't be able to see the roads to drive home."

Emma led them to a less crowded spot on the dance floor where they could hear each other better.

"It's all right, Granddad. That's what I have headlights for. Do you remember all the safety features we looked at when we picked out the car?"

"I know, and that's good, but there could be drunk drivers or hijackers. At this time of night, all sorts of delinquents come out looking for trouble."

Emma turned her wrist enough to see the hands on her silver watch. "Nope. It's just past eight-thirty. I think the murderers wait until at least ten."

He missed her sarcasm. "Murderers! I didn't even consider them."

"If you're ready to go, Granddad, we'll at least have to find Taylor and West and give our congratulations."

"Oh, yes. And please check on the card I put on the gift table. I'm so afraid it will get lost surrounded by all those big boxes."

"Of course. I'll make sure it's still there."

The song ended, and Emma took Granddad's arm, leading him to their table and putting his ice water glass in front of him. "Let me see if I can bring Taylor to you. I'm sure she'll want to say goodbye before they leave for Jamaica."

"So far away."

"It's only a honeymoon. We'll see her as much as we ever did when they get back." Emma's heart gave a painful squeeze, wishing she believed the words herself. Taylor and West had bought a house two hours away, near his new job.

The beautiful blushing bride was chatting with two of her aunts, but she came right over when Emma explained that Granddad was ready to leave. Taylor and Granddad had a special bond, and not just because she'd been his live-in nurse all these years. Even after he recovered from his stroke, Taylor stayed on. Granddad liked her company. She made his dinner just the way he liked it. She ironed and starched his shirts to perfection. Who would do that now? Certainly not Emma. It was easier to think those kinds of tasks were beneath her than admit she'd be terrible at them. It was too stressful to think about at the moment.

Taylor linked arms with Emma as they slowly made their way through the packed ballroom, often having to stop for people wanting to congratulate the bride or gush about her gorgeous A-line lace gown.

"How will you ever get back to West?" Emma asked.

3

"He'll find me." Taylor glanced around and spotted her new husband dancing with his grandmother. Her eyes softened with obvious love and affection.

Emma couldn't help feeling a swell of pride. After all, she'd brought the two together. Who knew matchmaking could be such a powerful thing?

Taylor moved forward and knelt in front of Granddad's chair, taking his hands. Emma automatically adjusted the back of her friend's dress to avoid making creases and stood by to make sure no one stepped on the end of it.

"Standing guard?"

Emma glanced over her shoulder at George. "Well, of course. It's part of the girl's code. We go to the bathroom in herds, pull loose hairs from sweaters, and hold up the ends of each other's fancy dresses. There's a whole list, but I'll spare you."

"And I appreciate that. So, are you and Mr. Woodhouse leaving? Could I possibly get a ride? Your sister and my brother are staying to the bitter end, I just know it."

"Of course they will. And if I wasn't such a homebody, I'd have you drive Granddad home and I'd stay. But as it is, my feet hurt, and all I want to do is curl up on my soft leather couch with a book."

"Then it's settled."

The three of them gave their goodbyes to Taylor, and George carefully helped Granddad through the crowds and out to the parking lot while Emma followed close behind.

At least if they were losing Taylor, they still had George. He stopped by almost daily to chat with Granddad and tease Emma about pretty much anything she happened to be serious about at the time.

It used to make her so mad—this brother of her brother-in-law who insisted on hanging around, not quite family and not quite friend. But now it was a game they played. Who could annoy each other the most? It took a lot to break George, but she was getting good at it. And she had a great new idea that was sure to drive him insane.

"Thank you for giving me a ride home, Mr. Woodhouse,"

George said to Granddad as they stopped to let a few faster-moving guests pass by on the sidewalk.

"Sure, Georgie. It's no big thing."

Emma shook her head at the way they greeted each other. Grandad was the only person who ever called him Georgie, as if he were a little boy. And yet, George still called him Mr. Woodhouse. She'd asked George about it once, and he'd only shrugged and said he wouldn't use Granddad's first name unless he asked him to.

George looked so tall and broad next to the stooped little man he escorted. The two continued to make small talk, with George nodding in agreement to all of Granddad's worries as they popped up. Emma admired George's long tan neck against the white of his shirt, his wavy hair just starting to curl under. He'd cut it soon. He always did. One of these days she'd find a non-weird way to run her hands through it before he cut it all off again.

Emma shook those thoughts away. She was happily single. Thinking of George that way was just ... odd. They'd fallen into a comfortable friendship, and anything more would mess everything up.

When they were in range, Emma used the key fob to start the car, which was always kept at a comfortable sixty-eight degrees for Granddad. In Burbank, California, that wasn't hard to maintain.

George opened the passenger door for Granddad, and then ran around and opened the driver door for Emma.

"Always the gentleman," Emma said before getting in.

"A thank you would be nice," he quipped back.

"Thank you, George."

He shut her door and ducked into the backseat where he stretched out, letting out a long, satisfied breath, and undid his top button.

"Such an introvert," she said, slowly shaking her head at him in the rearview mirror.

"Like you're not."

She pressed her lips together. Honestly, it depended on her mood. It would be awfully hard to be in the house with just

Granddad now. She should have found a replacement for Taylor right away, instead of putting it off. But how did you replace someone who was both the perfect friend and the perfect employee?

Granddad's eyelids were already beginning to close, though they opened wide for a moment as she went over a speedbump in the parking lot. Poor tired man. By the time they reached the freeway onramp, he was out cold.

George leaned forward between the two seats. "What did you think of Taylor and West's first dance?"

He wore the best cologne, and she took a second to breathe in the scent of him. "My official statement is that it was sweet and fun. Why? Surely, you're not one to criticize."

"They danced to 'You're the One that I Want.' I was hoping to catch your reaction, but I couldn't find you in the crowd."

"Well, you would have been disappointed. I smiled and clapped along with everyone else."

"What a good friend you are."

It was said with such sarcasm Emma couldn't help rolling her eyes at him. "Taylor and I have always chosen to disagree on *Grease*. I think it's the worst movie ever made. She will eternally love it. End of story."

It was the perfect response to cut him off at the knees. Besides, George hated the movie as much as she did.

"So," she said, trying her best to be casual. "I think I might get a little more serious with my matchmaking, now that I know how good I am at it."

"Ha!" George slapped the seat next to him. "Who have you matched up?"

"Taylor and West for one. He could barely talk to her when he came over to the house that first time. And then the silence would draw out and he'd get up and leave. Once I knew Taylor liked him back, I made sure to keep the conversation going, to find reasons for them to have to spend time together. I'm pretty sure the first time they kissed, it was while they were running errands for me."

"That is the worst recommendation speech I've ever heard, Emma. They already liked each other. How is that matchmaking?"

"Sometimes romance needs a little nudge. Oh, wow. I should write that down."

"It's a good tagline, but that's a terrible business idea for you."

Emma waved him off. "I already have a job. Helping the fashion-challenged is my passion and always will be. Matchmaking would just be a hobby to bring happiness to the romantically-challenged." She'd done it again. "Bringing happiness to the romantically-challenged," she repeated. "Oh, I am killing it tonight. Write that one down for me too. I should have gone into advertising."

George laughed. "Now that you have some great one-liners for ad copy you'll never use, can we get back to what makes you think you're qualified to match people up?"

"It's not just Taylor and West, you know. The whole reason we're stuck with each other is because I made my sister go out with your brother six years ago. She planned to cancel their date and stay home to study that night. But I *made* her go out with him because they were perfect for each other, even if she couldn't see it yet. And now they're happily married with two adorable children and one more on the way. What better success story is there than that?"

"Emma, I say this with no offense intended. I can't think of anyone less qualified to be a matchmaker. You've never been in love."

"And you have?" She narrowed her eyes at him in the rearview mirror.

George gave her one of his long, disapproving stares. He was very good at them. "No, but I'm not trying to be a matchmaker."

"Like I said, I'm not turning this into a business. Heaven knows I'm busy enough as it is. I'm just saying, if the opportunity presents itself, I'm not going to turn a blind eye. The world needs me."

George dropped his head in his hands, and Emma took the opportunity to giddily grin before returning to a face of serious determination. She'd succeeded in driving him completely mad, and all it took was two minutes and a wild idea.

And who knew? Maybe she'd actually get the chance to make another couple outrageously happy.

CHAPTER 2 ♥ BRIBERY AND BINGO

Bingo was in full swing at the retirement center. George sat next to another George, sixty years his senior, and took a bingo card from the stack.

"How're you feeling, George? Any side effects with the new medication?"

"None at all. I don't feel so nauseous after I eat now." The older George gave him a scrutinizing look. "Shouldn't you be on your lunch break, young man?"

"I am. I ate my sandwich on the way over." He pointed to B11, which his older friend had failed to cover. "Sorry, I'm distracting you."

"It's all right. They're giving out yoga balls as prizes again. I'll have to go in for hip replacement surgery if I try out one of those."

Actually, that was sort of a strange prize to give out to people with balance issues. He'd have to talk to the bingo lady.

Specializing in aging care began as a smart career move, but turned into a passion for him, as hard as it was to treat people in the last stages of their life. This retirement community was pioneering something new, keeping a primary care physician on site, and he was happy to be a part of it.

George glanced around, looking for his twelve-thirty appointment. Loraine had a history of not showing up, but they really needed to keep on top of her insulin management. She hated doctors, though George was doing his best to change that.

One thing Loraine never missed, however, was Monday Bingo. He spotted her at the table behind him, studying her bingo card like it might hold the keys to eternal youth.

He slid into the seat next to her before someone else took it. Loraine didn't look up from her card, but he didn't miss the scowl that crossed her face.

"You and I have a date in about thirty minutes, Loraine."

"I'm quite aware. And as exciting as it is to have a stalker, whether I come is up to me, Dr. Knightley."

"I'm a physician assistant. You can just call me George."

Loraine waved away his answer as if it were a bad smell in the room. "I'll call you what I like. How often is that overseeing doctor actually there?"

Pretty much never, but they were getting off topic. "It's true, nobody is forcing you to come, but maybe we could help each other out. George, over there, was telling me he's not a fan of these yoga balls they're handing out. I was thinking of using my influence to get some better prizes. Any suggestions?"

Loraine raised an eyebrow at him. "An all-expense paid trip to Fiji."

"Come on, Loraine. You know I'm not above bribery, but we have to stay in the realm of possibility here. What about the Friday afternoon dances? I hear they keep playing the same Beach Boys album because that's what the DJ likes. Is that true?"

"Yes. Beach Boys and the Four Seasons, week after week. Personally, I'd love a little Lionel Richie or Barry Manilow. Is that too much to ask? But no one listens to me."

"I'm listening."

Loraine shook her head while she placed another chip. "It doesn't matter anyway. I'm not dancing. I go because I like to watch the other fools."

"Are you wearing the compression socks we talked about?"

She lifted up her pant leg in answer. "Yes, I am. And if I'm hearing you right, we have a deal. Promise me you'll change up the music, and I'll show up for my appointment today. Now buzz off while I win one of these yoga balls so I can send it to

10

my granddaughter."

***

Emma had interviewed four people in one morning and knew there was zero chance she'd hire any of them. And that was before they had to pass Granddad's exacting scrutiny. Everything felt hopeless.

They weren't even trying to find a live-in nurse, just someone who could come weekdays and spend time with him. His anxiety was manageable with medication and someone there to rely on. Hiring someone with a handle on basic household chores would be a big bonus. Emma winced at the thought of her incompetence.

An early morning attempt to master ironing had ended with disaster. That shirt was hidden in the outside garbage, followed by a frantic run to the dry cleaners where she paid extra for same day service. She'd have to sneak out later and pick them up, discard the plastic covering, and take off all the tags.

Granddad could never know his clothes went to another location to be pressed. The horror. Years ago, a dry cleaner had lost a pair of his pants, and ever since, he had no trust in the business.

As a personal shopper, Emma worked with fussy people on a daily basis. Makeovers came with a lot of personal baggage and expectations. But none of her clients came close to Granddad. Emma felt like she was only beginning to see the tip of the iceberg of what Taylor had done for him.

Two more nurses were interviewing after lunch, and Emma looked over their resumes while she unpackaged the takeout sandwiches she was trying to disguise as homemade. Granddad wouldn't be fooled, but she hoped he would be placated by seeing it arranged on his usual plate with his usual silverware.

Her phone on the counter buzzed with a text, and she quickly brought Granddad his food at the dining table before running back into the kitchen to check it. Her clients knew she was taking some personal time, but that didn't mean she wanted to ignore any new requests they might have.

11

How's the matchmaking going?

Oh, it was only George. Her shoulders relaxed, and she leaned against the counter as she gave a tired little laugh.

Great. You reminded me to get started on it. I'd almost forgotten.

The fate of most of your grand ideas, unfortunately.

Not this one. I can guarantee it. So, know of any nice old ladies who are great at ironing and cooking and want to talk to Granddad all day?

Oh, Emma. Hang in there.

His answer was like a hug through her phone. Working at a large retirement community all day, George knew better than anyone how she felt. But he was never patronizing about it.

"Emma, aren't you going to eat something?" Granddad called.

"Yep. I'll be right out."

She quickly texted back: *You up for a couple more episodes of Cooking with Strangers tonight?*

Wouldn't miss it.

She put away her phone and took the resumes and her plate to go in and eat next to Granddad.

"This is good," he said, pointing at his sandwich. "Is it from that deli Taylor used to take me to?"

"Am I in trouble if I say yes?"

Granddad smiled. "Not at all. It's good of you to put up with an old man like me."

Emma instantly felt guilty for her frazzled text to George. "You and Granny raised me. There's nowhere else I'd want to be."

"What about when you get married and start your own family, like Isabella?"

Emma shook her head. "I'm twenty-four. There's plenty of time to worry about that later."

Grandad harrumphed. "I'm holding you back. Promise me you won't wait on account of me."

"I promise." They were placating words. She would not leave Granddad to fend for himself, no matter who came along.

He put on his reading glasses and reached for the resumes Emma had set aside. "More interviews today?"

"Yes, both of those." She wanted to take the papers out of his hand before he could read them over, but she held her hands in her lap.

"Harriet Smith. She sounds British and matronly. I'm not sure how I'd feel about that."

Emma ate a chip and suppressed an eye roll. "I'll meet her and find out. You, meanwhile, are going to watch Jeopardy. They put another season of it up on Netflix."

Granddad tilted his head down, looking at her over his glasses. "I should be helping with these interviews."

"You'd be helping me by exercising your brain and relaxing, rather than fretting over who's coming over. If I like them, I'll bring them in to meet you, and we'll go from there."

He looked like he wanted to argue further, but he dropped it and went back to eating. If they didn't find someone soon, the deli around the corner would be getting a lot of their business.

They finished lunch, and Emma had just settled Granddad with his show in the den when the doorbell rang. Right on time, which was one point in the person's favor.

Harriet Smith, it turned out, was neither matronly, nor British. In a soft southern accent, she introduced herself, and her kind, shy smile put Emma at ease. Emma gestured for Harriet to come in and follow her to the office. They sat in chairs across from each other, and Harriet fiddled with her jean purse before setting it under her chair and sitting up straight.

She was dressed in an electric blue, pleated skirt paired with a white button-down shirt under a hot pink cardigan. And bobby socks with tennis shoes. Clearly, she enjoyed fashion but also didn't care about what was fashionable. Interesting.

With thin, blonde curls that kind of fluttered around her cherub face, she looked like a little kid trapped in an adult body. Emma snuck a glance at her resume one more time.

"You're a registered nurse?"

"Yes. I finished my schooling last year, and I've been working at the hospital, but ..." She hesitated. "I have plantar fasciitis, and the doctor says if I work on my feet all day it will make recovery impossible. I'm as flat-footed as a duck so I have orthotics now, and I do exercises…" She trailed off, and her cheeks turned into patchy, red blotches. "I didn't mean to gab on, about my health problems. I'm very competent and hardworking, and I'm great with older patients. Does your grandfather like someone who talks a lot or would he prefer a quiet person? I swear I can be either of those things."

Emma hid a smile. Harriet was the worst interviewee of the bunch so far, and yet Emma couldn't help liking her.

"My granddad spends a lot of time worrying about things. He would do best with a calm and positive person who could redirect his thoughts to more interesting subjects."

Harriet beamed. "Oh, that's me. I'm sure we'd get along."

She was definitely positive. That was a good start.

Emma pulled out the sheet under Harriet's resume and handed it to her. "What about cooking and cleaning. Are you okay with the list there with your feet hurting?"

Harriet nodded, though her cornflower blue eyes carefully scrolled down the list, reading every item. She finally put the paper on her lap and gave Emma a curious look. "Can I ask why the pay is so good? I've been looking at similar positions for weeks, and most of them don't pay even half of what you're offering."

It was something Emma was quite aware of, and yet Harriet was the first person brave enough to ask.

"Granddad turns ninety next month. I want his last years to be with someone devoted to him, someone who will stick around. The last thing he needs is a revolving door of caregivers as his health declines." Emma watched Harriet carefully. "If your feet get better, say, in six months, will you go work somewhere else? Please be honest."

Harriet bit her lip. "With this pay, and if your grandfather and I hit it off, I'd definitely want to stay for as long as you needed me."

Emma gave an inward sigh of relief. "Follow me. Granddad is in the den. I'll introduce you."

CHAPTER 3 ♥ THIS KITCHEN IS GETTING HOT!

"So, you found someone. Congratulations." George leaned across the kitchen counter with his can of Dr Pepper and clinked it against Emma's glass of lemon water.

She eyed his soda can, looking judgmental.

"Stop it. Of all the vices I could have, one sugary drink every now and then is pretty tame." Though every now and then had turned into multiple cans a day. He'd think about that later. "Tell me about Harriet Smith."

Emma's face lit up. "She's perfect for him. Soft-spoken, but chatty, and eager to please. We start her one-week trial tomorrow to see if they suit each other, but I'm optimistic."

"Does she live nearby?" George salted the popcorn as it poured out of the old fashioned popcorn maker on the counter. Mr. Woodhouse was convinced microwave popcorn would kill them all, so Emma never bought it.

"Yes. Ten minutes west of here. It's perfect." She put down her glass and threaded her fingers together. "There is one thing worrying me about her, though."

Of course, there was. "Let me guess. She needs a makeover."

Emma scoffed. "Well, yes. But I only makeover people who want it. Self-confidence is the most important part of fashion, and I can tell Harriet likes what she wears. I'd never want to mess with that."

Self-confidence was an attractive feature. And an irritating one. All George had to do was glance at Emma, so comfortable in her own skin that he couldn't help wanting to occasionally shake things up, open her eyes to things beyond her own opinion.

Her thick blonde hair, always so carefully done up, was now hanging down her back, and it swung back and forth as she moved around the kitchen. He had to stop watching her so much. They were friends. He was six years older.

When his brother married her sister, Emma was just beginning her freshman year of college. Back then, she'd been a mouthy, opinionated, freckled, skinny thing who liked to tease. If he let that picture of her go, what would he see in its place? He wasn't ready to go there. Maybe he never would be.

"Hey, quit thinking about medicine for five seconds and help me carry this into the den." She smiled as she handed him the popcorn bowl, and then balanced the two plates of various snacks on the palms of her hands like a diner waitress.

They settled everything on the coffee table, and she woke up the TV and went through her list of saved shows until she found Cooking with Strangers. It was actually kind of flattering that she hadn't watched any episodes without him. Emma loved this stupid show.

"So, what's worrying you about Harriet?" he asked.

"She's named after Harriet Tubman, isn't that cool?" Emma took a few kernels of popcorn and chewed them slowly. "If I ever have children, I want to name them after important figures in history. I just decided this today."

George sat back in the leather couch and groaned. It felt nice to finally stretch out. "I'm named after George Washington, but I promise you, in elementary school I would have given anything to be one of the three Ryans or Michaels in my class."

The show announcer started his spiel. *"They thought they were here for a blind date reality show. Little did they know they'd have to work together as couples, using their prowess in the kitchen for a chance at splitting half a million dollars. Ten weeks. Ten meals. Will they fall in love, or kill each other in the process? This kitchen is getting hot!"*

16

George picked up the remote and paused the TV. "Okay, hang on. You totally avoided my question."

"What question?" Emma was staring at the paused TV as if she could turn it back on with her eyes.

"About Harriet. You know what, never mind." It wasn't even that he wanted to know. It was the way Emma had stepped around it that had him curious, as if she wished she'd never introduced the topic in the first place.

Emma bit her nail and then pulled her hand away and sat on it. She'd been trying to kick the nail biting habit for years. "She has a serious boyfriend who just moved to Reno, Nevada."

"Ahh. You're worried she'll move there to be with him?"

"Yes. But let's not talk about that right now. I want to see if Donny and Denise will admit their feelings for each other."

"They ruined their pasta last episode. If they can't even make pasta, they're done."

Emma looked at him as if he'd just admitted to treason. "But they're my favorite couple. They can't go."

Her investment in this show was hilarious. She looked visibly shaken at the thought of losing Donny and Denise. Every episode began with an elimination so that they could end the show on a cliff-hanger question of who was leaving next.

Emma unpaused the TV and settled back, threading her arm through his and resting her hand on his bicep.

Sometimes he wanted to just ask her: Did she not consider their friendship odd? Their increased cuddling lately odd? But he didn't ask, because he liked the feel of her tucked in next to him, whether intentional or not.

"The couple leaving us today is ...." The host took a couple of cleansing breaths and shuffled the papers in his hand.

George gripped her knee. "Cue the dramatic music and lighting. Dun, dun, DUN!"

"Oh, stop." Emma laughed, ruining her attempt at irritation. More over-the-top pauses ensued while Emma shushed him for making fun of it.

"Tenisha and Leif, you've been eliminated."

"No!" Emma wailed.

"Why are you upset? Donny and Denise are safe."

17

"But I liked Tenisha and Leif's fighting. So much sexual tension going on there, and now we'll never know."

"Are we even watching the same show?"

Emma's lips gave a cute little pout. "She's the sassy city girl, he's the hick with the mad cooking skills. You know their parents would hate each other. They had a whole racial Romeo and Juliet thing going on. It was fascinating."

George rubbed his eyes. "Stalk them on social media then."

"I will, but they needed more time together. Now they have a long distance problem."

On the show, everyone was hugging and saying their goodbyes. It wasn't fair to eliminate them since they had actual cooking talent. They just happened to have an undercooked dish on the last challenge. Why was he analyzing this? Dang Emma had sucked him into this, too.

"Who are you rooting for, George?"

"Since I hate all of them, I'm always happy when anyone leaves."

She raised an eyebrow. "Then why are you here?"

There were so many possible answers to that question, none of which he wanted to share with her. He used to leave after Mr. Woodhouse went to bed, but the past few months he'd been staying and hanging out much later than that. "I like the actual cooking part, you know, when they're not sneaking off to make out."

"Yeah, that part's a little icky when they know cameramen are like two feet from them."

"No different than actors. It's all acting. None of the romance on here is real, you know."

"You don't know that," Emma said quietly. She took a big handful of popcorn and ignored him, focusing on the show.

She wanted it to be real. It wasn't fair to steal that for the sake of teasing her. The last thing he wanted was to suck the enjoyment out of it. Annoy her to death, yes, but never make her truly unhappy.

He knew Emma was dying to return to work, but she'd chosen to spend the last few days with Mr. Woodhouse and search for caregivers. She deserved a little downtime to think about something else, however frivolous.

The five remaining couples prepared sushi while the large clock on the wall counted down their remaining time. Donny and Denise did seem to have a certain synergy in the way they moved around each other, calmly divvying up responsibilities. Neither of them had much cooking experience, but they definitely tried the hardest.

"I guess I'll root for Donny and Denise, too."

Emma turned and stared at him, probably gauging whether or not he was making fun of her. He must have passed some kind of test because she scooted closer and leaned against him again.

"You're a good egg, George."

Definitely a friend kind of statement, and not a romantic one, which was for the best anyway.

There was a soft knock at the door, and Emma paused the show.

"You expecting someone?" he asked.

"No. It's probably Elton. He used to come over all the time before Taylor met West. Poor guy. I think he was a bit in love with her."

Hardly. George wasn't sure Elton was capable of loving a person as much as he loved ideas and the genius of his own mind. Elton was writing yet another book on ancient religions and likely needed a study break. Emma was the only neighbor he had under the age of sixty-five.

Emma put down the popcorn bowl and jumped up to get the door.

"Check the peephole, Emma."

She saluted in agreement before leaving the room.

After a few seconds, Elton's soft chuckle echoed from the front door, followed by Emma's gentle shushing. Mr. Woodhouse would be anxious about guests over if he woke.

Elton strolled into the den first and eyed the TV. Even at this time of night, he was dressed in slacks and a pinstriped dress shirt, paired with a skinny tie. "This? This is what you two are watching? Dr. Knightley, I have to admit I'm shocked."

It wasn't the first time Elton had called him Dr. Knightley.

There was no point in correcting him again. At this point, it was mockery, which was better left unacknowledged. Elton was not a threat to him, physically or intellectually, though he might think of himself as one.

Emma sat next to George, and Elton joined her other side, helping himself to the popcorn. It was a tight fit for three, and George wondered what bothered him more, that he wanted Emma all to himself or that Elton seemed to feel the same way. Neither would concede the loveseat to the other and go sit on the couch alone with the bad view of the TV. He wondered what Emma would think of their unspoken tug-o-war over her.

"When is Taylor getting back?" Elton asked.

Emma tossed George a knowing look before answering. "She and West return next Saturday. But then they're packing up and moving to Santa Barbara. She's already found a job there."

Elton covered her hand with his. "I'm sorry, Emma. I know how much you relied on her."

George eyed Elton's bony hand and gave an inward sigh of relief when he removed it.

Emma, oblivious to the minds of men, as always, settled back against the loveseat and stared at the frozen screen. "You up for a little reality TV, Elton?"

"I suppose. My reading on the Eleusinian Mysteries can wait."

Emma cocked her head. "That's the one about ancient Greece, right?"

"Very good, Emma." Elton's ice blue eyes lit up in admiration. "You listen very well."

Emma couldn't resist a compliment. She blushed prettily and pretended to examine her fingernails.

George picked up the abandoned remote control and turned the show back on. "At this rate, we'll be watching this one episode all night."

Emma giggled. "George is eager to see what happens to Donny and Denise."

"Really?" Elton put an arm around the back of the loveseat, which no doubt would eventually make its way around Emma. "Which two are they? Are we rooting for them to win?"

George was glad Emma was the one to shush him so he didn't have to.

"Just watch, Elton," she murmured when he asked again. "The couple with the blue aprons."

"What's going to happen to them?" Elton asked.

They both shushed him.

CHAPTER 4 ♥ MY NIECE, JANE

Emma finished going over her work calendar and ran to get the door. Harriet was right on time for the second day in a row. With any luck, Emma could get back to wardrobe consultations by the end of the week.

"Good morning, Miss Woodhouse." Harriet's radiant smile matched her outfit today, a bright blue blouse with large red cherries all over it and bright yellow wide-leg pants. It went against everything Emma had ever taught people about blending colors or flattering their body type, but somehow on Harriet it all worked.

"Granddad is in here." Emma led the way to the kitchen, where Granddad was frowning at his runny oatmeal. Yes, Emma had eyeballed the amount of water needed. She'd never do it again. If only there weren't an infinite number of ways to mess up just about every domestic task.

"Let me see the bowl. I'll make you a new one." Emma took it from him and went over to the garbage to scrape it out.

Harriet went to the oatmeal container and studied the cooking instructions. "I can do that, Emma." She eyed the dirty pan on the stove where the leftover oatmeal was beginning to crust. "Can we not microwave it?"

Granddad looked up in horror. "It's terrible for you."

Harriet nodded. "I've heard that. But then if you would be so kind, Mr. Woodhouse, would you please get this pan soaking

22

while I get out another one?" She scraped the excess oatmeal into the garbage before putting it in the sink for him. It wasn't as if she couldn't turn the faucet on herself. But that wasn't the point.

Emma hid her surprise and watched Granddad out of her peripheral.

Granny had waited on Granddad hand and foot until the day her heart gave out. A week later, he'd had his stroke, and they thought they might lose him, too. Taylor was heaven sent, and at the time, Emma hadn't questioned the way Granddad relied on his nurse for just about everything. Taylor had helped him regain his independence in walking and bathing, in getting dressed, and getting in and out of chairs. But everything else, she'd done for him, meeting his every need the moment he'd asked.

Harriet didn't wait for a response from him. She opened one of the lower cupboards, looking for a clean pan, and Emma directed her to the correct shelf. They both faced the stove and exchanged furtive glances while Harriet prepped the new batch of oatmeal.

The scrape of Granddad's chair and his slow shuffle to the sink had Emma frozen in place, waiting. When the water came on, Emma let go of the breath she'd been holding. Amazing. Simply amazing.

***

George took a real lunch break, as his next appointment would definitely not need to be tracked down. Betty Bates was the sweetest woman on the planet, and the chattiest. She lived with her frail mother in one of the community apartments and found joy in everything around her, from the weekly bingo games to the baked goods one of her neighbors often brought over. Medically, there was nothing wrong with her except slightly elevated blood pressure, so they often just chatted after he checked her over. The only thing she needed was more human contact, and not the kind from friendly checkups every few months. He wished the rest of her family would come see her, instead of sending letters and cards.

Betty had decorated a whole wall of their apartment with the cards from her nieces and nephews. As Mrs. Bates, Betty's mother, was too weak to come into the clinic, he visited her there. He'd gotten to be friends with both of them, more than any of his other patients.

George balled up the foil wrapper from his sandwich and took out his phone to check the time. Emma had sent him a dancing emoji. He imagined that meant things were going well with Harriet and Mr. Woodhouse.

Good day? He texted.

Amazing! Twelve stars. Harriet has Granddad sorting socks with her while they watch TV.

Well, good for her. Well done, Emma. Sounds like you picked a winner.

Emma wasn't the best judge of character, hence why she didn't mind Elton hanging around, but she also had unusually good luck. Finding Taylor was the perfect example of that. George was curious as to which camp Harriet fell into, and he wanted to meet her. There was an incredible amount of trust given to a caregiver who stayed in your home day after day, and he wanted Emma and Mr. Woodhouse to be in good hands.

When George returned to the office, he went over his schedule and decided to leave right after meeting with Betty Bates. Dr. Perry was actually there for once and agreed to handle the afternoon appointments.

You mind me stopping by this afternoon? I hear there's a leaky faucet calling my name.

Emma responded right away with a whole line of thumbs up. George put his phone away, washed his hands, and went into exam room four to see Betty Bates.

She stood as soon as he walked in. "Oh, George. You'll never guess what has happened. My niece, Jane, is moving to Burbank this week, and she's coming to stay with us while she looks for an apartment."

George was genuinely happy for her, and let her gab on while he checked her vitals. "Hold on, Betty. I need you to take a few deep breaths and not talk for a minute." He listened to her breathing and her heart. Everything was as it should be.

"Why is your niece moving here?" George asked. He knew Betty was eager to talk about it again.

Betty's face lit up. "She's such a talented girl. The medical practice where she was a receptionist closed, and she'd just broken up with her boyfriend. It was time for a change, she said." Betty grabbed his arm. "George, do you think she could be a receptionist here? You haven't put up a sign asking for a new receptionist, but I know yours has been in bad health for some time, and you've been doing most of it yourself."

Actually, Lois, their billing specialist had stepped in, but Betty was right. Lois didn't like the extra work and had balked at taking on more hours than she was already doing. Their receptionist wasn't just missing days, she'd been out for weeks, and had officially turned in her resignation yesterday.

Still, he did not want to get Betty's hopes up, only to have them dashed. Hiring friends or even acquaintances could get messy.

"I'm sure she can find a position, Betty. She'll be all right."

Betty wrung her hands together. "I know, but I read the community bylaws. If she works a full-time position within the retirement community, she'd be able to live with us. Otherwise, she'll have to leave after two weeks, whether she's found a place or not. We could save her so much money. I could move into Mother's room, and she could have the other bedroom."

George placed a steadying hand on Betty's shoulder. "Just enjoy her visit. Anything else is full of maybes that would pressure her into trying to please you and her grandmother."

"You think so?" Betty slid off the paper-covered table and turned to straighten it out. "So, you think I'm meddling too much?"

"Betty, I don't know what kind of relationship you have with your niece, but if it was me, I'd reassure her she's welcome to stay and then let her figure out the rest. You can tell her about the position, but after that, let it go. Starting over often means choosing something completely unexpected. Maybe Jane doesn't want to be a receptionist anymore."

"Oh, that makes sense. Thank you, George."

Only an angel like Betty could take such advice without offense. Their conversation turned to her diet and exercise, which somehow turned into a dinner invitation for when Jane arrived.

George didn't have the heart to tell her no, but he hoped in all the excitement of her niece coming that she'd forget.

CHAPTER 5 ♥ FIRE OR NO FIRE

"Come in!" Emma recognized George's three quick knocks. After he'd texted he was on his way, she'd unlocked the front door.

He closed the door behind him and met her in the kitchen where she was carefully cutting up a carrot. She would not mention how close she'd come to slicing into her finger in the process.

The sound of the *Jeopardy* theme song filtered in from the den, and they both turned to look at the backs of Harriet's and Granddad's heads.

Granddad moaned. "Oh, I hate this chatting part after the first commercial break. Alex Trebek is so condescending, and the contestant's answers are an embarrassment. The combination is just …"

"Awkward," Harriet filled in for him. The two laughed together like they were the best of friends.

Emma rolled her eyes. "When he's crotchety, she only laughs harder. Maybe it's a honeymoon period, but they are a match made in heaven."

"What are you making?" George asked.

The carrot slid out from her knife again, and she pulled her hand back just in time.

"For the love of your fingers, Emma, put the knife down."

She huffed out an embarrassed breath and set the knife on

the counter.

"Sorry." He leaned in until she had to look at him, and his expression was a mixture of sympathy, and amusement, and just a hint of mischief. "Dangerous with a knife—you can add it to your resume."

"Uh, no. I won't be bragging about my knife skills, thank you. This is between you and me. Forever."

George crossed his heart. "I won't tell a soul. But, can I show you how to cut carrots without losing any vital body parts?"

He washed his hands, and then came and stood shoulder to shoulder with her. "Try cutting at an angle, like this." He rocked the knife back and forth like a pro, and little oval slices lined up one by one. "That way, the knife is never riding on top like a teeter-totter."

He made it all seem so simple. And it was true. It didn't matter what shape the carrots ended up. She kind of liked the ovals anyway.

"Can you picture us on *Cooking with Strangers*?" She laughed as she took the knife from him and slowly began making more ovals. "We'd be eliminated the first night after I set our meal on fire."

George shrugged. "I think they'd like you enough to keep you around for a couple episodes, fire or no fire."

Their eyes met, and she willed herself not to blush, because her mind had immediately gone to an image of her and George skulking in a corner with their lips locked together, cameras forgotten. Okay, that show was messing with her head. If George knew she had thoughts like that he'd probably stop coming over. Time for a subject change.

"How do you feel about cutting onions?" she asked.

George picked up the onion on the counter and stuck it in the freezer.

"That good, huh? I guess we won't be having onions with the roast tonight."

He leaned against the counter so they were facing each other. "You'll cry a lot less if the onion is cold when you cut into it."

"Oh. I was about to order onion goggles online," Emma

admitted.

"That doesn't surprise me one bit." He stole a piece of carrot as he studied the recipe book on the counter. "Do you have a garlic press?"

"No idea." She gestured toward the utensil drawer and went back to chopping carrots into careful little ovals.

Harriet came and stood in the doorway.

"Oh, George, come here for a second." Emma turned him around from the utensil drawer, and he and Harriet shook hands over the counter. "Harriet, this is my old friend, George. George, this is Granddad's new nurse, Harriet."

Granddad shuffled in and surveyed the mess on the counter. "We may need to order out," he whispered to Harriet, though everyone heard him loud and clear.

Harriet slipped her an apologetic look. "Oh, no. Emma has this handled, don't you?"

"Of course, I do. Granddad, could you show George the leaky faucet in your bathroom? He's agreed to take a look at it, and we should hold him to it before he comes to his senses."

Granddad nodded enthusiastically. "Yes, Georgie, come see. I don't want some strange repairman in my bathroom. He might steal my blood thinner medication and try to sell it on the black market."

Emma waited until the two had left the room before asking, "How are things going?"

Harriet shrugged. "I like it here. Are you ... happy with me?"

"Very much so. You're doing great."

It was not a conversation that could be elaborated on. Everything was in wait-and-see mode. Harriet had cleaned the bathrooms and mopped the kitchen during Granddad's nap today, but when he was awake, she would relax next to him and just be there. Emma couldn't ask for more than that.

The only thing making Emma nervous was the constant exchange of text messages and FaceTime calls between Harriet and her boyfriend, Martin. Granddad didn't seem to mind. They often included him in their conversations. It was Emma who didn't like it. Long distance relationships were not meant to remain long distance forever.

Not that she wanted to spy, but she'd been taking careful account of Martin's good and bad qualities in the bits she'd overheard, putting them up against hypothetical men Harriet could date here in Burbank.

After all, if Emma planned to continue her matchmaking streak, she might as well start where she could do the most good.

On her cons list was the fact that Martin's hair was continuously greasy and dirty. He'd pull off his ball cap, run a hand through it, and then stick the disgusting cap back on. Also, he was an over-the-road trucker, so even if Harriet moved to be with him, he'd constantly be away from her. He also made corny jokes and often allowed long pauses in their conversation as if he didn't have a thought in his head. Harriet needed someone with better communication skills.

To be fair, on the plus side, he seemed very attentive, maybe to the point of being an annoyance, and he was big on compliments. He always told Harriet how pretty she was and how much he missed her.

"I think that's enough carrots," Harriet said with a little laugh.

Emma looked down and realized she had indeed peeled and cut up the whole bag during her contemplation.

Harriet picked up the cutting board and slid the carrots into the roasting pot around the roast. "It's very nice of you to make dinner for us, Emma."

"I want to help while I'm here."

"Itching to get back to work?" Harriet asked.

Emma nodded.

"So, you do wardrobe makeovers? Is that right?"

"Yes, that's part of it. We go through every item of clothing they own and get rid of what's not working. Then I take the client to a store that matches their needs and help them pick out clothes they'll actually wear. If I do my job right, it saves them time and money, and they feel more confident about how they look."

"That's fabulous. You said that was part of it. What's the other part?"

"I have some regular customers, mostly older ladies who ask me to shop for them. I know them well enough to know what they like, and I have relationships with stores so I can bring items to their homes, let them try them on, and then return anything they don't want. Sometimes I do online shopping for them as well."

Harriet sighed. "That's it. I've decided I'm going to be you when I grow up, Emma."

***

Thanks to a quick run to the hardware store and a couple of YouTube videos, George had the leak in the bathroom fixed before dinner.

Emma called them to the table, all official-like, and George slid into the empty chair next to Harriet. She'd been staring at her phone, but she quickly put it away and glanced around as if reacquainting herself with reality.

"Hello again," she said, smiling at George. "Did you figure out the leak?"

"I did. I almost feel handy now." He glanced across at Emma and shared a small smile with her. "Usually I have to beg my brother to come help me. He got all the mechanical skills in the family."

"Oh, I'm sure that's not true." Harriet tipped her head in sympathy. "Though I know what you mean. My boyfriend, Martin, taught me all sorts of maintenance things for my car, but I'm not sure I'll remember them when I'm stranded on the side of the road. Although, there's always nice men who pull over and offer to help before I can even get the jack out of the trunk."

"Do you break down a lot?" Mr. Woodhouse asked in alarm, hugging the salad bowl Emma had been passing around.

Harriet laughed. "Any car, new or not, can get a flat tire."

Mr. Woodhouse still looked concerned, but Emma distracted him by asking him to pass the salad bowl and offering him dressing.

"Emma," Harriet said, putting down her fork. "Since you're

so good with fashion and all that, I wanted to ask what you thought about my hair. I've been wanting to dye it red for oh, so long, but I'm too scared to do it. Do you think I should?"

George focused on his salad, knowing Emma wouldn't brush it off with a vague 'you go girl' type answer. He wasn't wrong.

"Um, so there are a couple problems with blondes going red. Sometimes it turns out pinkish or orangey, so it's important to tell the stylist exactly what type of red you mean and make sure she knows what she's doing. Also, it's very light sensitive, so there's a whole regimen for keeping it brilliant between colorings."

They continued to discuss it in detail, with Emma giving her expert advice and Harriet eating it up like a late-night bowl of ice cream.

George took it upon himself to serve up the roast, and then read off the newspaper Mr. Woodhouse insisted on keeping by his plate at dinner. It was a habit Emma had unsuccessfully tried to break him of.

Harriet left right after they ate, and shortly thereafter, Mr. Woodhouse got ready for bed. He usually fell asleep to CNN, which Emma would shut off later.

Emma turned her bright eyes on George as soon as the two of them were alone. "So, what did you think of Harriet?"

He turned on the water to start the dishes. "I think she's great. She seems like a very happy person." He didn't want to say it, but the way Harriet had skipped out the door with her phone to her ear, told him a lot of that happiness came from the guy on the other end. And for someone who worked one-on-one in caregiving, outside relationships were important.

Emma scraped the plates and handed them to him one by one, occasionally flicking him with water and clearly enjoying his exasperation.

"What does your sister think of her?" he asked.

"Isabella hasn't met her yet, but she and the kids are coming over Thursday to visit with Granddad." Emma dropped her head. "I hope it goes better than last time."

"Good luck with that." Granddad was not great with children, especially ones as free-spirited and boisterous as

Isabella's. It didn't help that he had a lot of breakable things on display. Their last visit resulted in the demise of his rose-glass candy dish. "Hide the breakables this time."

Emma stuck her hand under the faucet and flicked him with water again. "Johnny climbed up on my desk and spider-monkeyed his way to the top of the bookshelf. How was I to know three-year-old's could do that?"

"I think a good rule would be to assume nothing is impossible with that kid." George wiped his wet hand down her arm as she set the roast pan into the sink, and she squealed and backed away.

She rubbed off her arm and made a face at him. "I almost forgot to tell you. I've decided on my first matchmaking candidate. Do you want to hear who it is?"

"Nope." He turned up the water to full blast and made as much noise as he could scrubbing the roast pan until she ducked under his arm and wrapped herself around him. It was a good technique. She was very hard to ignore when she did things like that.

Batting her eyelashes up at him, she said, "Come on, George. Humor me."

He tucked an errant strand of hair behind her ear. "The roast turned out good."

"Thank you. I'm just glad nobody died from eating it."

"Yet."

That earned him a soft punch in the ribs.

"Please, George. This is important to me."

His shoulders dropped, and he reluctantly turned off the water. "All right. Tell me about your matchmaking." It was the last thing in the world he wanted to talk about. As far as he was concerned, matchmaking was a polite term for being a meddling busybody.

Unleashing herself from him, she bounced on the balls of her feet and clapped her hands. "Be excited for me. So, I was thinking I'd start with Elton. He spends so much time researching and writing, holed up in his house, but he's so good at flirting and compliments. He's even sort of handsome with all that chestnut hair and his slim, scholarly build. He just needs

33

someone to coax him out a little more."

"Nope." He picked up a hand towel and threw it in the air. "Nope. Nope. Nope."

Emma smothered a giggle. "You can't throw in the towel, George. You promised to listen to me."

"When? I don't remember promising anything of the sort."

"Um, when you said, 'all right, tell me about your matchmaking.'"

George rubbed his head. "That's before I knew who your first victim was with all his chestnut hair. It's brown, right? Or is there some girl nuance I'm missing?"

She cocked her head to one side. "There are lots of shades of brown. Your eyes, for example, are a rich, coffee color with a swirl of cream in the middle. A girl could get lost in them." Her mouth turned up slightly at her success in making him self-conscious. "Oh, George. You've distracted me with your good looks again. But back to Elton. Don't you think he deserves love?"

That wasn't a question he wanted to spend even two seconds considering. "Why don't we go watch *Cooking with Strangers*, or *Princess Wars*? Whatever you want. Just don't talk about Elton's love life. I beg of you."

He'd fallen right into her trap. He knew it the second she broke into a satisfied smile and dragged him into the den. She pulled a blanket off the back of the loveseat and laid it over the top of them, snuggling right into his side. In this case, it was a win-win.

***

Emma paused the show and listened for the light rapping noise she thought she'd heard. Yep, there it was again at the front door. She glanced at George, totally passed out, and couldn't help smiling. He hadn't made it ten minutes into Princess Wars, but he was a good sport.

She checked the peephole and then let Elton in. "Couldn't stay away, huh?"

"You're always up, and you do provide good snacks." He

34

rubbed his hands together. "It's kind of cold out there with that wind blowing."

"I could make some hot chocolate."

"I could definitely go for some of that." Elton followed her into the kitchen and sat on a stool. "I've been writing for five hours straight, and my eyes and back told me it was time to take a break. I'm up against a deadline, but my agent is really excited about this next book. He says it's my best work yet."

"That's awesome, Elton." Emma had no desire to read any of it, but she was happy he'd found something he was passionate about. Everyone deserved something like that.

She needed a way to ask him some matchmaking questions without making it patently obvious why she was asking. Luckily, she had time to think while Elton described in detail the different societies of the ancient world and what made them different from each other.

It wasn't that Emma didn't like history, but Elton tended to focus on the less interesting bits and use them as evidence for why religion was bad. While Emma wasn't particularly religious herself, it made her uncomfortable to hear him strip away things others held sacred. As a result, she usually tuned out most of what he said and just nodded at the right times. Elton had never noticed.

Taking down two mugs, she filled them with hot water from the glass measuring dish she'd just microwaved. Elton ripped the top off a hot cocoa packet and tapped it into his mug.

Using the lull in the conversation, she dove in. "So, Elton. Whatever happened to that girl you went out with last year? The one who drove the Maserati?"

He made a face. "We went out a few times, but she wasn't what I'm looking for." He smiled at that last part, and Emma tried not to let excitement fill her. That meant he was looking.

"In what way? What did she lack?" she asked.

"She wasn't genuine. I come from money, but I've chosen a quiet, scholarly life. I don't spend a lot on dates or clothes. I think she was expecting something different since she met my parents at their country club before they introduced us."

He was looking for someone genuine and down-to-earth.

That perfectly described Harriet. Emma hadn't told George this part, of course, but she'd decided if Elton and Harriet were to meet and hit it off, she wouldn't stand in the way of a good thing.

Emma shrugged. "I thought she was pretty, with her blonde hair and big blue eyes." His last girlfriend wasn't quite a dead ringer for Harriet, but they were both curvy blondes with a light smattering of freckles. Maybe that was his type.

"Why all the questions, Emma?" The corner of his mouth slid up, and he leaned forward.

From the other room, George murmured in his sleep.

Elton froze. "Was that your grandfather?"

"Oh, no. That's George. He fell asleep while we were watching TV."

Elton set down his mug and looked at his watch. "I'd better go. You may want to kick out that deadbeat, too. Doesn't he have to work in the morning?"

"Good point." Emma walked Elton to the door and then tiptoed into the den to wake up George and send him home.

"George, wake up."

He bolted upright from the couch, waving a combative arm in the air as if being attacked. Emma hid a laugh. It was a familial trait. Her sister complained about John doing the same thing all the time.

"George."

His eyes finally landed on her, and he broke into an embarrassed smile. "I didn't mean to fall asleep. How long was I out for?"

"Almost an hour. I've been having hot chocolate in the kitchen with Elton. He just left. You should go before Granddad finds out you tried to stay the night."

George smirked. "I'll take that bet. Your granddad hasn't been up past nine-thirty in twenty years."

"That's not the point. He has a strict house curfew, afraid rogues like you will take advantage of me."

He mussed his already adorably messy hair and grinned. "I'm not trying to stay the night, and I'm pretty sure I'm the farthest thing from a rogue you'll likely encounter."

"True." Emma sank back into the cushions and rested her legs over his knees. "I could fall asleep right here."

"Oh, no you don't. Come lock the door behind me before you go to bed."

"Don't you have a key?"

He yawned. "Yes, but you're lying across me, and now I want to stay here."

Their eyes met, and something passed between them that made her heartbeat pick up.

"Sorry, I'll move." She pulled her legs back and picked up the blanket next to her, folding it so her hands had something to do. She didn't breathe easy until George left, and she turned the lock.

CHAPTER 6 ♥ BANNED FROM CANDY

"Johnny, no!" Emma caught the sturdy toddler just as he launched himself off of Granddad's favorite reading chair. Destination: the glass-covered coffee table.

"Let me fly," he insisted, squirming out of her arms like a wriggling fish. The second his feet touched the ground he took off running.

In hot pursuit of him, Emma did a full loop around the dining table before she doubled back and caught him again. He was laughing, the infectious, carefree laugh of a child who knew he was being an absolute stinker. Emma couldn't decide whether to cry or laugh with him.

"Is everything okay in there?" Isabella called from the kitchen. She, Emmy, and Granddad were making sugar cookies. Bonding time, Isabella had called it. Johnny lost interest four seconds after they started, and Emma, the non-baker, was sent to keep an eye on him.

He needed more than an eye. More like two arms and a leg lock. How did Isabella keep up with him day after day? "We're fine," she called back. Sort of.

"Can I have candy?" Johnny asked, his bright face full of hope. "I like the red ones."

He was remembering the sweets from the candy dish, though apparently not the broken glass or angry adults.

"You're banned from candy here. Remember?"

"What's banned?"

He patted her cheeks and she leaned down and kissed his nose. "It means it's time to go outside and throw shriveled-up oranges at the wall."

He cheered, and she sagged with relief. Their orange tree was so big that the top fruit would inevitably remain unpicked, and after drying up to practically nothing, would fall down if the wind blew hard enough. After realizing Johnny was fascinated with them, she'd saved a bucketful for when he came over again. She took his hand and let him drag her out the back door.

While Johnny happily chucked the hard brown objects at their block wall, Emma pulled out her phone and called Taylor. She'd been trying to give Taylor honeymoon and new marriage space, but it was hard not to talk to someone Emma used to see every day.

"Hello?"

"Taylor!" Emma couldn't help squealing out. "How are you?"

Taylor groaned. "So good. Except for work. I hate it. You and Granddad spoiled me for all those years. I come home dead on my feet and immediately shower. If it wasn't for my awesome roommate situation, I'd hate it."

"Your awesome husband roommate?"

"Well, yeah. You should find one of those. I highly recommend it."

"Oh, yes, I'll get right on that," Emma said as sarcastically as possible, though her thoughts betrayed her and immediately conjured up an image of George with his beautiful, brown eyes.

"So, how is Granddad? Is he okay? Did you find some help?"

"I did, actually. Her name is Harriet Smith, and I love everything about her except for her long-distance boyfriend who calls multiple times a day."

"Ooh, that could be a problem. Is she gonna run off and get married like I did?"

"I don't think he's the one for her."

"Well, you would know. You saw West's potential before I did."

Johnny complained about Emma's lack of participation, so

she picked up a dried orange and threw it at the wall. Okay, throwing these things was sort of satisfying. She threw another one, and Johnny whooped, launching one into the air. She caught it before it landed on his head, almost dropping her phone.

"Are you still there?" Emma asked, putting her phone back up to her ear.

"Yeppers. Is that my Johnny I hear?"

"Yeah, I'll see if he wants to talk on the phone." Emma tried to coax him over to say hello to Taylor, but he was not interested. As far as he was concerned, if Taylor wanted to talk to him she could appear in the flesh. He loved Emma chasing him, though. He ran away giggling, and she followed him around the tree. At this point, she'd take anything that kept him entertained and out of trouble.

"Emma, if you don't think he's the guy for her, I think you should maybe discuss some phone time boundaries and see how it goes. She's either gonna get defensive real quick, and you'll know you have a problem on your hands, or you might open her eyes to maybe backing away from him. Sorry, I shouldn't butt in. It's totally not my place anymore."

"No, no. That actually makes sense. I'll think about it."

Harriet was coming later today, after Isabella's visit. Maybe Emma would find a way to bring it up, though she hated to mess with a good thing, and having Harriet there was definitely a good thing.

"Hey, I have to go," Taylor said. "You amazingly called me right at my break time. I'll call you soon, okay?"

Emma said goodbye and tucked her phone in her back pocket right as Johnny dropped a handful of oranges on the ground and kicked at them.

"All done," he said, waddling toward the house. His diaper probably needed a change. Isabella said potty-training with a new baby on the way was a lesson in futility. Having never potty-trained anyone, Emma was in no position to judge.

Emma ran and headed him off before he reached the door. "No, wait. We just need a target. Like a ... monster or something."

She ran over to the abandoned sidewalk chalk from the beginning of their visit and took a piece back to the wall. "Watch, Johnny."

She drew a hulking figure with three googly eyes and big teeth. A few extra strokes and he had hair spurting out in random places. Johnny pointed. "Moster."

"Yep, that's a monster. Let's get him." She stepped back and threw one of the shriveled oranges at the chalk figure.

Johnny joined her, and they kept it up for another fifteen minutes until Isabella called them in for cookies. It was the hardest earned cookie break she'd ever had.

***

Dr. Perry stopped George as he exited their exam room. "Hey, I've hired someone for the receptionist position."

"When?" Technically, it was Dr. Perry's job to hire people, but George hadn't expected him to actually get it done.

"This morning. She's very experienced and motivated to work here. I guess her aunt and grandmother live on the premises, and she's moving in with them.

"Betty Bates is her aunt, then?"

Dr. Perry's eyebrows rose in surprise. "You knew? Well, now I feel even better about it. She has some unpacking to do today, but she'll be coming after lunch for a little bit of training. Her name is Jane Fairfax."

"Sounds good." George wiped down his laptop and headed to go wash his hands and change his lab coat. His last patient had coughed all over him, and tests would probably confirm pneumonia.

There was no use worrying about the receptionist until he met her, but the whole thing struck him as odd. Jane had to be either extremely practical or extremely desperate to want to live in a tiny apartment with her spinster aunt and grandmother. As far as he knew, she'd never visited before, so her decision to move in with them wasn't out of love.

His curiosity about her stayed like a buzzing gnat through his next few appointments, until Jane herself came in the door and took off her sunglasses. She was younger and more attractive than he'd expected. He hoped that wasn't the reason Dr. Perry had hired her. Being recently divorced, Dr. Perry's bitterness had fueled a need to go through girlfriends like loads of laundry. An in-office romance like that would only end in disaster.

George went out to greet her and bring her into the back office. Her handshake was firm and her expression one of neutral interest. If she was nervous, she didn't show it.

"I'm George, the physician assistant. I'll take you to meet Lois, our billing specialist. I believe she'll be the one training you."

"Yes, that's what Dr. Perry said."

"Good. He's with a patient right now. I'm sure you'll see him later."

George walked her over to Lois's desk, and the old lady looked down her glasses and gave Jane a once over. He could see the same concerns registering in Lois's suspicious face about why Dr. Perry had hired this girl on the spot. Lois wasn't a person who stood for any kind of nonsense.

"This is Jane, the new hire. Jane, this is Lois."

Lois sniffed loudly. "All right, pull up a chair, girl. Let's see how you do with the scheduling software."

"So nice to meet you," Jane said softly. She rolled a chair over to the desk and sat, taking a pair of reading glasses out of the case in her purse. Once George saw that they weren't going to kill each other, he stepped out and went back to work.

***

The ironic thing about trying to talk to Harriet about her phone habits was that she showed up on the phone with Martin and continued their animated conversation while she collected Granddad for his daily walk. Emma didn't get more than a hello in before they left.

She sat at her desk and checked her email, responding to a few potential clients and adding things to her calendar while she waited. Harriet and Granddad were nothing if not predictable. Taking the route with the least amount of barking dogs, they'd circle back through the neighborhood and walk in the door in exactly twenty-two minutes, unless they stopped to talk to a neighbor. It was a walk Emma had taken with Granddad many times.

It wasn't just Taylor's advice that had her eager to talk to Harriet. Emma had two back-to-back appointments this afternoon, and starting tomorrow, she would return to working full time. Harriet's trial period was up, and while Emma was excited for it, she was also nervous. This afternoon would be the largest chunk of time Emma would spend away from Granddad since Taylor's departure. She wanted to go over emergency numbers and Granddad's morning medications. He did not like Emma's insistence that she check his pills to make sure he wasn't forgetting or taking the wrong ones.

Emma glanced at the time and then checked outside. Right on schedule, they were coming up the driveway. She opened the door and smiled at the sight of them, one insanely cheerful and the other insanely grumpy.

Harriet beamed at Emma. Her cheeks were rosy from the exercise and her hair blown all about. "What a glorious morning."

Granddad harrumphed. "We made it back alive. I guess that's good." He headed straight for his armchair and picked up his beat-up John Grisham novel from the side table.

Harriet's phone jangled with Martin's signature ringtone, and she gave an apologetic smile. "Hang on, we already had our morning chat so this shouldn't take long."

"Martin," she scolded, turning away from Emma and walking into the kitchen. "Did you forget to tell me something?" She giggled at his response. "Well, I know that. You tell me every day. I love you, too."

Emma resisted the urge to roll her eyes. Of course, he wasn't calling for any particular reason, but the two of them would draw it out forever. Emma put her computer to sleep and picked up her phone. She had about ten minutes, give or take, before traffic would prevent her from being on time for her meeting.

Gathering up her things, Emma peeked her head in the den,

but Granddad was already snoozing in his reading chair, the paperback open on his chest, rising and falling with his deep breathing.

There was nothing to do but stand in front of Harriet until she got off her infernal phone. The silent hint worked. Harriet said a final goodbye to Martin and stuck her phone in her back pocket.

"Does he call you every morning?" Emma asked, trying to sound casual.

Harriet pressed her lips together in a nervous gesture. "Well, not every morning. But most mornings."

"Even though he knows you're working?"

Harriet's eyes widened. "Oh, I'm sorry. Do you not want me to take personal calls?"

"No, it's fine. I just figured he'd worry about getting you in trouble." It was an honest criticism. Why didn't the guy fear getting his girlfriend fired with all his calls? Or perhaps he was hoping that would happen so she'd move near him.

"I'll have him cut it back, I promise." Harriet turned and opened the dishwasher, letting out a puff of steam. She gathered up the clean cups and bowls as if her job depended on it.

Emma walked around the island counter, feeling bad for making Harriet think this was about neglecting her job. Harriet was doing all she asked and more. "Harriet, relax. You're allowed some downtime. That's not what I was saying. I just wonder if maybe there's something else that brings you joy, besides reassuring Martin that you miss him. Like a hobby." *Or a less clingy boyfriend.*

Harriet paused with the bowls in her hands, her forehead wrinkling as she considered Emma's suggestion. "I'll have to think on that. I have been neglecting my crafting lately. I used to knit hats for cancer patients."

"What a great thing to do. I think I even have yarn tucked away somewhere from when I tried knitting once. I was horrible at it. I'll go look for it, but first, let's go over Granddad's pill schedule. And did you see this emergency phone list over here? Do you know everyone on here?"

Harriet gave her a sympathetic smile. Emma knew she must

44

sound like an anxious mother leaving her baby with a sitter for the first time, but she wanted to make sure Harriet had everything she needed. Once that was out of the way, Emma retrieved her abandoned yarn and knitting needles from the top shelf of her closet and handed them off to Harriet.

"Tell Granddad I love him. I'll be back in a few hours."

Harriet shoed her away with a wave of a knitting needle. "We'll be fine."

CHAPTER 7 ♥ LET'S PUT A PIN IN THIS

The client, Laurel Hathaway, looked in dismay at the get-rid-of pile on her bed. To her, it represented money wasted. But Emma knew that gut clenching regret was a good feeling to have. It meant forever after, Laurel would only buy clothes she'd actually wear, clothes that made her look and feel good.

Emma folded up another reject and lightly tossed it onto the pile. Laurel, afraid of her height and curves, had been hiding behind shapeless sweaters for too long. This was L.A. Nobody really needed a heavy sweater here, shapeless or not. "I have a great charity if you'd like to donate them."

Laurel nodded. "Okay. Okay, I can do this. What's next?"

"Let's make a wish list. We definitely need something to match those pinstriped pants you wear to work."

It felt so good to get back to this. Cleaning out cluttered closets was the one domestic task Emma excelled at. And from the hundreds of closets she'd seen, it was obviously a struggle for a lot of people.

Together, they made a detailed wish list and an appointment to meet again in three days for a shopping trip. Emma took the huge pile of discards off Laurel's bed before she had a chance to change her mind and stuck them in the back of her car. She'd drop them off at the shelter on her way home.

Laurel kept her house at North Pole temperatures, and Emma took a minute to defrost in her sun-warmed car before turning it on and driving home.

The house looked the same as when she'd left, and Granddad was in his usual chair yelling Jeopardy responses at the TV, so all was well.

Emma hung up her purse and walked around until she found Harriet in the kitchen, scouring the sink with such fury Emma was afraid to interrupt.

"How was it?" Harriet asked, not bothering to turn around.

"Just fine. Is everything okay?"

Harriet nodded, but the hunch of her shoulders told a different tale.

"Harriet?"

It all came out in a flood. "Everything is a mess. Martin and I talked this afternoon, and I told him we couldn't be on the phone as much anymore, and he apologized and got really quiet. And when I pressed him on it, he said he missed me so much, he won't be able to stand it if I don't move there soon."

Emma's throat tightened. This was exactly what she'd been trying to prevent and all she'd managed to do was hurry it along.

Harriet whirled around and dropped her rag on the edge of the sink. "I don't know what to do, Emma. I just started here, and I promised you I'd stay."

Time for some damage control. Emma took a deep breath, willing her thoughts to stop racing. "He's breaking up with you if you don't move to be near him?"

Harriet shook her head vehemently. "No. We're not breaking up." She sniffed and fanned at her face, but it was no use. The tears were already threatening to storm.

"Well then, don't cry. Give it some time and think about what you want to do."

"I always cry when someone says not to." Harriet wheezed out. "I don't know why." She wiped at her eyes, but it only smeared her eye makeup across her cheeks. "You're not mad at me?"

Emma pulled a packet of makeup remover wipes out of her purse and handed one to Harriet. "I want what's best for you. So, let's work through this. Martin's on the road all the time, no matter where you live, right?"

"Well, not all the time, but a lot."

"So, what does he expect you to do when you move there? I don't see this getting any better. Are there nursing jobs in Reno where you could be on the phone with him all the time like you are here?"

"Probably not."

Emma handed Harriet a tissue next, and the girl blew her nose.

"So, you either live with a long distance relationship, or the two of you decide it's not going to work." That was a little harsh, but then the situation sort of called for it.

Harriet twisted the tissue in her lap. "Yes, I see your point. Don't worry, Emma. I will figure this out."

"I know you will." Emma's confidence was all for show. Inside, she was a churning mess. What were the chances of getting another great nurse to replace Harriet? And how long would that take? Emma's business couldn't handle another long hiatus.

What Harriet needed was a distraction. A good one. A chance to meet someone without realizing she was there to meet someone. It seemed callous to plan something that would sway Harriet in favor of staying, but it was for everyone's good. Matchmaking required a little bit of maneuvering, even a little nudging sometimes. Harriet would be better off without a long distance relationship, and then she'd be open to new possibilities, like Elton. But how was she to help Elton and Harriet fall in love without revealing her role as matchmaker?

They needed to meet in a low-pressure environment with plenty of chances to talk. Harriet was here every day, but being in caregiver mode, her focus was on Granddad, and she wasn't dressed to impress.

Emma whipped out her phone and Googled possible date ideas until she came across a post about murder mystery dinner parties. They sold kits online with instructions and costume suggestions. All she'd have to do was host it.

It was the perfect way to make sure two specific people were seated next to each other and interacting without being conspicuous about it. She'd invite Isabella and John, of course.

It would give them a fun date night that didn't revolve around Netflix after the kids went to bed. They didn't get out often enough. George would hate it, but he'd come because he was a good sport.

Emma would have to carefully add other single people to cloak the fact that she was playing matchmaker for Elton and Harriet. Everything was coming together. She had a plan.

***

Who else is going to this thing?

George watched the little dots indicating that Emma was working on an answer to his question. He considered possible motives behind Emma's sudden need for a dinner party. Emma never did things like this without a goal in mind. That's just how she operated.

Who are you, a mean high school girl? You don't ask who else is coming before saying yes.

Oh, Emma. Being elusive about the guest list was not a good sign. Chances were pretty good he'd cave and go to this thing, but not before giving her a hard time. He looked at the clock on the wall. He had about two minutes left to get some real information out of her, or at least frazzle her in the process.

And yet, I'm asking.

You're the first to know. You should be flattered I'm telling you before everyone else.

Ah, a guilt trip and deflection. That wouldn't work on him. He'd let his non-answer percolate while he checked with his brother. Chances were pretty good Isabella was in on this new scheme, and she and John didn't keep secrets from each other.

John had the big, rough hands of a construction worker, and he hated texting. He said it was for teens with no social skills. Unfortunately, that usually meant phone calls where they shouted to each other over the sound of a band saw whining in the background.

Sure enough, when John answered, there were lots of hammering and clattering tool noises going on behind him.

"Hey, John, did you and Bella get invited to some murder

mystery dinner party by Emma?"

"Yeah, not happening. Not if I have any say in the matter."

"Is that a yes or a no?"

"I guess that's a no, I haven't heard anything. But I'll check with Bella. Dang, she'll want to go to that, won't she? Never get married, George. It's a trap."

George laughed. John and Isabella had their own twisted sense of humor when it came to their marriage. There were no two people in the world more in love, and yet they used nicknames for each other like 'hope smasher' and 'dream killer.' Weirdos.

John hung up, and George went back to his text message thread with Emma. He wouldn't be able to check his phone again until he left work, so he typed out a quick response sure to spin her up.

So flattered. Let's put a pin in this and talk about it in five years.

She'd love that. Now that he thought about it, his relationship with Emma was as weird as Isabella and John's.

He put his phone away and approached the reception desk.

He knew from the way Lois audibly sighed every time he came within five feet of her, that training was the last thing she wanted to be doing today. Frankly, it was the last thing any of them wanted her doing, but someone had to see patients, so she could continue to sigh away if it made her feel better. However, the paperwork he'd let pile up could no longer wait, and he brought it to the desk Lois and Jane were sharing and cleared his throat. Lois kept typing, but Jane whirled around.

"Can I help you with something?"

He handed over his stack of request forms. "These three need pre-authorizations from insurance and these are referrals for specialists. I need them all before the end of the day."

"I'm on it," Jane said.

His phone dinged with another text message, but he didn't check it. Persistent little Emma would have to wait.

Jane sifted through the forms. "Oh, Aunt Betty wanted me to remind you that you're invited to dinner this Thursday at six. She's making meatloaf, and it's better than it sounds. You're coming, right?"

"I … Yes, I'm coming." Somehow saying no to Jane was as impossible as saying no to Betty Bates. Between this and the murder mystery dinner, his social life had revived from a near death experience. Was there anywhere to run from pushy females? His life seemed overrun with them lately.

Lois motioned for the papers in Jane's hands, and she reluctantly gave them up.

"Make dinner plans another time," Lois said, waving the stack of papers at Jane. "We haven't gone over cancellations yet, and while you're up, I need you to look up in that top cupboard and get me a roll of receipt paper." Lois turned her shrewd eyes on George and crooked one long bony finger at him. "And not so fast, young man. Mrs. Wallis in 108 had a fall last week and ended up in the emergency room. She's coming in for a follow-up, and you'll need to go fetch her from her apartment and wheel her back here."

"Yes, ma'am," he and Jane chorused at the same time. They shared a look of long-suffering before each went to do Lois's bidding.

***

Emma woke up full of ideas for her party. Yesterday, she'd managed to get an enthusiastic yes from her former college roommate, Nicole, and a promise to be at the dinner party from her college friends, Austin and Cara. They were all single and fun at parties. As a bonus, this was turning out to be a little college reunion of sorts.

Taylor and West couldn't make it, which was a bummer. But with Granddad resigned to participate in it and Elton and Harriet both excited to come, Emma could finally go into full planning mode. While still lying in bed, Emma called up Isabella and reminded her to get a babysitter. Her sister could be flighty about such things.

"It's already done, Emma. And it's my good babysitter. She actually keeps the kids alive and does the dishes."

"So glad to hear it. You and John need to get out more."

"Doesn't everyone? Don't worry about us. It helps my sanity that we put the kids to bed at seven every night. Oh, speaking of. Emma, did you tell Johnny a scary story about monsters or something yesterday? Last night he kept pointing at his bedroom wall and whispering, 'monster.' It took forever to get him to go to sleep."

Emma went from feeling like the best aunt ever to the worst. "Well, I did draw a monster on the wall outside with chalk, but he was a friendly one, like a Sesame Street character." Except for the sharp teeth. That was a mistake. Emma ran her knuckles up and down her forehead. "I'm sorry. I did the best I could to keep him entertained. I didn't think the kid was afraid of anything."

"Don't worry about it. Now that I know what it was from I feel much better. Sometimes he and John Senior watch movies I'm not happy about, so this has happened before, only last time it was battle robots with shiny eyes keeping him awake."

"Men."

"When are you getting one of those, Emma?"

"A man? Are we having this conversation? I swear Taylor asked me the same thing yesterday."

"Come on. What about George? He hasn't had a serious girlfriend in almost a year. Ever thought of putting a move on him?"

Emma would not answer that question. If Isabella knew Emma had even an inkling of interest in George in that way, she'd never let it go. "Serious is right. He always picks women way too serious for him."

"Exactly. He needs someone a little bit silly."

"I'm choosing not to be offended by that."

Isabella laughed. "Well, good for you. I meant it as a compliment. And remember it's not just us married people who need to get out more. I love that you're so good to Granddad, but make sure you get out of that house occasionally, too."

"Duly noted. If you need help with your costumes, let me know." Emma said her goodbyes and crossed Isabella's babysitter off her to-do list.

As she dressed and did her makeup, Emma considered what

decorations she'd need and what to buy now that she'd settled on a roaring twenties theme. Everything was coming together.

Bothering George with questions about it was fun in its own way. She usually didn't pester him at work, but in order for her to assign out characters for the murder mystery, it required RSVPs. His response to whether he wanted to be Mayor Graft or Mr. Peabody was *whichever lets me show up in a tee-shirt and jeans.* Not happening. She'd pick out his costume herself, twirly mustache and all.

***

George almost didn't hear his phone with his music up so loud in the car. He liked to listen to movie scores, and this morning it was *The Last of the Mohicans.* Turning it down, he picked up his phone and accepted the call from John.

"What'd you find out?" George asked.

"We're going. Isabella got a babysitter, and I talked her out of ordering me a costume, but I have to wear a suit and tie. She's gonna murder me when I spill food on it." This morning it was the sound of giggling and shouting children in the background John had to yell over.

"Okay, but did Isabella say why Emma decided to have this party?"

"Because she thought it would be fun. That's what Isabella said."

"Seems like a lot of work for fun."

John laughed. "That's what women do, George. They complicate things that should be simple." He let out a roar and must have grabbed up one of the kids because the squealing and giggling got louder. "Sorry, man. I don't have any super-secret information for you. But if I have to go to this thing, you better be there, too."

George pulled into the parking lot of the clinic and parked in the back. "Yeah, I'll be there. See ya."

He hurried into work, knowing his first patient would probably be waiting for him.

Lois and Jane were at the desk running through the morning

53

scheduling routine. Hopefully, by the end of today, Lois could return to her billing desk and leave Jane to handle things on her own up front. They didn't look any happier to be sitting next to each other than they did yesterday.

George listened to them talk as he studied his patient's case history.

"Why did you move here?" Lois asked. "Dr. Perry said you had a good job in Sacramento."

When Lois got comfortable around people, she'd start asking pointed, personal questions of them, and follow those up with questions meant to trap the person in their half-truths. Nobody told Lois the full truth about themselves. She didn't invite that kind of candor.

Dr. Perry flat out told the woman to mind her own business when she tried it on him. Lois only cackled in response. You couldn't offend her on purpose. If she wanted to take offense, it had to be on her terms.

Jane shifted in her chair. "I did have a good job. It was just time for a change."

Lois scoffed. "People only say that when things go wrong. Nobody wants a change from the good things in their life."

"Good point, Lois." The dry humor in Jane's voice indicated that she was about done on the subject. "Am I supposed to click anything here before I go back to the main screen?"

"Yes, you have to save all this." Lois took over the mouse and demonstrated. "So, what went wrong?"

"With what?" Jane asked.

"With Sacramento. Was it family problems? A vengeful coworker?"

"Are you planning on being a vengeful coworker?" Jane asked.

Lois let out a huff. "No, I was being hypothetical."

Jane was good at deflection, he had to give her that. His patient came up to the desk with paperwork, and Jane was saved from further questions. For the moment.

George remembered what Betty had said about it, that Jane left a bad relationship to move here. She deserved to keep that to herself. He certainly wouldn't be sharing the little information he knew.

"So, why did you need a new start?" Lois asked when the patient sat back down in the waiting area. "Money problems?"

George slid over in his roller chair. "Lois, could you check and see if the new insurance covers the generic or the name brand of these three medications listed here?"

She gave him the stink eye, knowing it wasn't urgent, but not quite insolent enough to challenge him on it. "Of course, dear."

Jane sent him a grateful look, one person with secrets to another. Lois liked to interrogate George about his dating habits from time to time, always with disapproval and unwanted suggestions, regardless of whether he had a girlfriend or not. He'd found it was better to avoid answering at all.

CHAPTER 8 ♥ A SMALL LOVESEAT

George held out a spring flower bouquet to a delighted Betty and came into the tiny apartment. A smiling Mrs. Bates was sitting at the table, and George felt horrible for ever trying to duck out of coming to dinner. Anything that motivated the little old lady to get out of bed was worth a little awkward dinner conversation.

"Jane, he's here."

The sing-songy way she said it had George worrying this was some kind of date set-up, but Jane came out of the back bedroom with a guy in tow, and George was both relieved and concerned all over again. There was a reason the community was strict about their age requirements for residents. The mystery of why Jane wanted to live in this retirement villa and be bullied by Lois all day was still beyond him.

"Hey, I'm Finn Churchill, Jane's friend." The guy swiped a lock of his overgrown, sun-bleached hair out of his face and held a hand out for George to shake.

"George Knightley. Nice to meet you."

"Come sit down, you two." Jane motioned to the chairs on either side of her, and they complied, sandwiching George between Jane and Betty.

"Finn surprised Jane today with a visit. I don't think I've ever seen anyone more surprised. Would you agree, mother?" Betty patted her mother's hand, and then, noticing the straw for Mrs. Bates's water cup was still in its wrapper, she tore it open and helped her mother take a small sip with the straw.

"A good surprise, I hope." Finn grinned at Jane.

She slowly waved one hand back and forth in a meh kind of answer, which had them elbowing each other and giggling.

Betty smiled. "It's so refreshing to have young people around. Finn is staying for two whole weeks. It will be so nice. For all of us."

"Staying here?" George couldn't help asking. The apartment wasn't big enough for a full couch. There was a loveseat tucked against one wall with the TV opposite, but as it was, George could probably lean out from his chair in the kitchenette and touch it if he wanted to.

Finn shook his head. "Oh, no. I'm staying at my Dad's place. He lives like ten minutes from here."

Betty jumped up when the oven timer went off. "I have to get the rolls out. Jane, dear, would you mind serving up the meatloaf? Start with mother's and cut it into small pieces for her."

Jane jumped up to help, and George did too, after scooting in to let Jane by. Finn just sat there, his eyes following Jane in an amused sort of way. George decided to withhold judgment until he knew the guy better. After all, there could only be so many helpers in a tiny kitchenette.

"Is this too much?" George asked Finn, placing a plate of mashed potatoes and meatloaf in front of him.

"Nah, man, this is great." Finn beamed at Betty when she brought the basket of rolls to the table and handed them to him first. "You're the best, Aunt Betty."

Betty turned five shades of red and carefully sat down to eat with them. The soft clanking of forks filled up the space for the next minute until Betty patted her mouth with a napkin and turned to George. "You're single, aren't you, dear?"

Jane put a staying hand out. "Don't answer that."

"Well, I was only wondering if he could introduce you to his circle of single friends, Jane. I'm not trying to set him up." Betty patted George's arm. "I'm not trying to set you up."

"I am single," George admitted. "But I think you overestimate my social circle." His phone chose that moment to ding with an incoming text message. He should have remembered to put it on silent.

"Who's that then?" Finn asked, nodding at George's phone with a mischievous grin. He seemed like the type who lived for a good joke.

"Yes, who?" Betty chorused, rubbing her hands together.

George pulled his phone from its holder and swiped it open. "This is from my friend, Emma. She's pestering me about the costume party she's having next Friday."

"A costume party?" Betty's eyes lit up as if he'd announced they were all going to Disneyland, and a highly impulsive idea occurred to George. He tucked it away for later contemplation.

"We're not even close to Halloween. Why is she having a costume party?" Finn asked, leaning back in his chair.

"It's one of those murder mystery dinner parties, with a roaring twenties theme."

Betty's eyes grew even bigger. "Oh, Jane. Can you imagine? Wouldn't you like to go to something like that?"

Jane shook her head. "Not really."

Betty's shoulders dropped. "But Finn's leaving in a few weeks and you don't want to rattle around here with Mother and me."

Jane shot Finn a sly look. "I'll be fine. Don't worry about me."

George was relieved when the conversation turned to other things besides his or Jane's social lives, or lack thereof.

During the break between dinner and dessert, George texted Emma back, letting her know he'd be over later. If she insisted on including him in party planning, he had a request of his own.

***

Emma glanced at the clock, wondering what time George meant when he'd said 'later.' He was late enough to miss Harriet leaving and Granddad going to bed. She'd already turned off CNN on Granddad's TV and tucked the covers around the snoring man.

Maybe it was a good thing George didn't see Harriet though. The girl wore her heart on her sleeve, and at the moment, her heart was aching over what to do about Martin. Emma hated watching them try to pick up the pieces of their disintegrating relationship. They were at an impasse. Harriet would not quit her job and move, and neither would Martin.

Emma was trying her best to be impartial about the whole thing. But it was hard to be impartial when the decision would determine whether Granddad had a nurse or not.

Either way, Emma was resolute in going through with the dinner party next Friday. She'd already talked Harriet into coming over early so they could get ready together. She'd chosen Harriet's role carefully. As Kitty Darling, Harriet would wear a twenties-era flapper dress and maintain a mysterious, yet flirtatious, air. The style flattered Harriet's short blonde hair, and with dramatic makeup, she'd be irresistible. The dress Emma had bought for her was amazing. Elton would never be the same.

There was a light tapping at the door, and Emma tiptoed over to check the peephole and let George in.

"Hey, stranger."

"Hey, yourself." She swallowed hard as she looked up into his dark eyes. It seemed like every time she saw him lately, there was an electric charge to the air, something crackling and unspoken happening between them that made her feel like if she didn't grab hold of something, she'd lose control.

Emma did not like to lose control of anything, especially not her feelings. She escaped to the kitchen and opened the fridge. "Someday I'll have to give up this late night eating. You want to watch something and have some chocolate pudding with me?"

"Sure."

She focused on getting out bowls and spoons and serving them up. Handing one bowl to George, she led the way into the den and sat against the armrest on her side of the loveseat. Pulling a blanket over herself and draping it between them, it almost seemed like less of a gulf. Almost. Cuddling just wasn't the natural friendly thing it used to be. Now, it made her want things she shouldn't want. They'd always been friends. Becoming more than that could ruin the perfectly good relationship they already had.

George didn't test her on the extra space between them. He sat on his side and rolled out his neck. "I was invited to dinner by one of my patients."

"Are you gonna go?" Emma asked.

"I already did. It was tonight."

"Do tell." Emma listened to him talk about some woman named Betty and her aging mother while she scrolled to her saved shows and found their next episode of *Cooking with Strangers*.

"Wait, who is Jane?" she asked, trying to keep track of names in his story.

"She's my new receptionist and Betty's niece." He picked at the ties on the blanket. "Would it be okay if I invited Betty to your costume party? I think it would be the thrill of her life."

Emma paused the TV. "I guess that would be fine." George so rarely asked for things that Emma couldn't help agreeing. And the more people who hid the true purpose of the party, the better.

The various character roles still available scrolled through Emma's mind. She had the principle people already assigned, of course, but the kit allowed add-ons as needed. "Do you think she'd want to play the nosy neighbor or the down-on-her-luck dancer?"

"I'll ask her, though I don't think she'll care. I have a feeling she'll try to weasel an invitation out of me for her niece too, but I don't think Jane will accept. If Betty insists, would you have room for Jane, too?"

Emma poked him in the side. "Your 'one more' is starting to get complicated. Didn't you say Jane's friend was staying for the next two weeks? Will he want an invite? What about Betty's mother?"

"I'll get back to you on that." He smiled in a way which said he knew exactly how annoying his request was.

Emma turned the show back on. It was elimination time, and she scooted a little closer to George as the camera focused in on

Donny and Denise, their favorite couple. They looked like they knew this was their episode to go.

"They've been so distracted by each other that their cooking has gone to complete crap," George murmured.

On the screen, they were doing a flashback montage of previous dishes and kitchen mishaps, like the time Donny oh so slowly wiped flour off Denise's cheeks while their pie overbrowned.

"Is that a good sign or a bad sign in a relationship?" Emma asked. "When all you can think about is the other person, and when you're with them you forget about everything else?"

George's eyes left the TV and slowly turned toward her. His gaze darted to her lips, and a tug low in her belly warned her something was happening. She both desperately wanted it to happen and was terrified by the possibility.

George slid his fingers around a lock of her hair as he came in closer. "Emma," he whispered. His lips looked soft.

"What?" The little word came out in a puff of air between their mouths.

A soft knock sounded at the door, and she jumped as if stung by a bee. The remote rolled off her lap, and she dove for it and paused the TV on a jubilant Donny and Denise. Somehow, they were safe for another week. She'd missed it.

"That sounds like Elton, doesn't it?" George asked. He was studying his hands with deep concentration.

"Yeah." She escaped the den, taking deep breaths in the foyer until she felt calm enough to answer the door.

Seeing Elton's oblivious smile on the other side filled her with a sudden urge to slam it in his face. But that was insane. This was better. A buffer person was most definitely in order.

"Come on in. We just started an episode of *Cooking with Strangers*." She led him into the den, and as much as she wanted to plop him right in the middle of her and George, that would have made things awkward in a whole different way. Nope, she had to be in the middle. It was a small loveseat, with barely enough room for the three of them, but the best view of the TV. Perhaps she should rearrange the furniture. She'd have Harriet help her with that tomorrow.

Emma tossed the blanket she'd been using back into the basket, suddenly feeling warm and claustrophobic, and tried not to notice the way she was brushing up against both men's arms. Of course, all the sensations were firing on George's side.

"I should make popcorn. I'll be right back." She jumped up and left the two men alone while she zipped around her kitchen, finally remembered the popcorn, and then, with the bag in her hands, stared at the microwave as if she'd never seen numbers before.

She kept a secret stash of microwave popcorn bags. George didn't even know about it. Sometimes, there was nothing like the salty, buttery taste of three-minute convenience in a bag.

When she returned to the den with the bowl of popcorn, both men visibly relaxed. She knew Elton was not George's favorite person, though he'd never said anything specific in that regard.

"What did I miss?" she asked.

"One of the couples making out. We fast-forwarded it."

"Which one?"

They both shrugged.

"Does it really matter?" Elton asked.

It totally mattered, but she'd go back and catch what she missed later. She didn't want either guy's summary of it anyway.

Elton reached for a few kernels of popcorn as Emma squeezed between them again.

"So, who else will be at this murder party?" Elton asked.

George snorted, though it was so quiet, Emma was sure Elton missed it.

"Well, for the dinner party, there's you and George, me, Granddad, and his nurse, Harriet. You haven't met yet, but she's fabulous. Then there's my sister and brother-in-law, my friends, Nicole, Cara, and Austin. Oh, and a friend of George's named Betty."

Elton counted on his fingers. "That makes eleven."

"For now." Emma glanced at George. "We might get one or two more. Shhh, shhh." She fluttered her hand at Elton before he could ask any more questions. The judges were about to make the rounds and look at everyone's dishes.

Emma willed her mind to focus on the show and not on the feel of George's thigh against hers or his hand occasionally brushing against her leg. But her hormones had other plans. She could have sworn she blinked and the show's closing music played.

Elton stood up and stretched. "George and I should get out of your hair. After all, a party planner needs her sleep."

"True," George responded, not leaving the sofa.

The two seemed to be having some kind of tense staring contest, but when they caught her watching, they knocked it off. Guys were strange.

She picked up a stray popcorn kernel and followed them out to the kitchen. George gave her a small side hug and left without a word. And what was there to say? *I almost kissed you. Maybe we should talk about it.* Nope. He'd have to bring it up first, and knowing George, he wouldn't.

Elton cleared his throat, breaking her trance. She'd been staring at the door ever since George had walked out of it.

"You and George have known each other a long time."

She nodded. "Yep. His brother married my sister."

"Really?" Elton's jaw dropped. "So, the two of you are like, in-laws."

"Yes."

"But, you're not … together."

"Oh, no." Emma turned away so Elton couldn't read her conflicted thoughts on that subject. She closed the microwave popcorn box and put it in her hiding place in the top of the pantry, moving things back in place so even Harriet wouldn't find it. "Elton, I'm excited for you to meet my friends at this party. Cara and Nicole are hilarious, and Harriet is the smartest, sweetest person I know. Really down-to-earth and gorgeous."

"I'd love to meet your friends."

Emma turned and almost knocked into him at the entrance to the pantry. "Well, good. I think it will be lots of fun. Let me get you your costume guide before you go." She moved around him and got it out of her party planning binder. "If you've already put something together for Mayor Graft, that's okay. I just thought this could spark some ideas."

Elton took the guide from her and tapped it against his hand. He seemed to want to say something more, but he turned and walked to the door. "Good night, Emma."

"Good night, Elton."

CHAPTER 9 ♥ THE BRIGHT SIDE HAS BETTER LIGHTING

Betty was in raptures over her invitation to the murder mystery dinner party, and as George predicted, as soon as she stopped gushing about how thankful she was to be invited, she asked if Jane was going. Which was why he'd stopped by Betty's apartment on his lunch break while Jane was at the office. Betty would have asked right in front of her niece and thought nothing of it.

"Betty, take this opportunity to get out and let Jane stay with your mother for once. Trust her when she said she wasn't interested."

Betty wrung her hands. "Oh, I don't know. I'm sure Jane would be a better fit for a party like that."

That reaction was what George had feared. Betty always thought of others before herself.

"Betty, I'm inviting you." George stared her down until she finally nodded. "If you want, I'll pick you up, and we'll arrive together."

"And you're sure it's okay with your friend, Emma?"

"I already asked her."

Betty bit her nail. "Then I'd love to, but what would I even wear?"

George showed her the two option pages with costumes,

and Betty chose the nosy neighbor wondering about the noise next door. She was supposed to wear curlers in her hair and slippers.

"Oh, this will work fine, I know it." She thanked George again and took the instruction sheet and invitation inside, humming to herself.

With that out of the way, George's mind was free to dwell on other things, like the fact that he'd almost kissed Emma, and she hadn't seemed too opposed to the idea. What he did with that realization was another thing entirely. Did they pretend it never happened? What if it happened again?

His mind took off with that possibility, and he stomped back to the office to the rhythm of NO, NO, NO, telling his imagination to dial it back in. He'd ruin their friendship and make family functions forever awkward if he was misinterpreting her signals.

Knowing he had to tell Jane she was staying with her grandmother while Betty went out definitely helped squelch any thoughts of Emma trying to linger. What if Jane did want to go? Would she be offended he didn't ask? He had back-to-back appointments, but before they closed, he caught Jane at the front desk while Lois was in the ladies room.

"Hey, Jane. Your Aunt Betty was so excited about my friend's murder mystery dinner on Friday night that I invited her. Would you mind staying with your Grandmother while she's gone? Or did you and Finn have plans?"

Jane didn't look particularly miffed, which was a relief. "Not any specific plans. We could stay in and watch a movie or something. I'll let Finn know." She pulled her phone out of the purse hanging on the back of her chair and opened her messages, starting to type something.

George didn't mean to be a snoop, but the last message between Jane and Finn was right there, and the words practically jumped off the screen. *Make up your mind about us.*

That was a little bold on Finn's part, though maybe Jane had been keeping him in the friend zone for a long time, toying with the guy when it was convenient. Okay, he was way overthinking something that was not only none of his business but not worth caring about. Maybe Emma's reality TV shows were getting to him.

***

Emma juggled the clothing store bags in her arms until she could reach a hand out and blindly stick her key in the lock.

Her latest client had done well with their shopping appointment, but being only five feet tall, some of the things they'd picked out for her had to be hemmed. Some clients could afford to let the stores handle that, but not everyone. Years ago, Emma had found a dirt-cheap, but high quality, alteration place in a strip mall next to a Chinese buffet. The only problem was their weird hours and propensity to not answer the phone.

After knocking on the shop's door with no success, Emma took everything home.

"Harriet? Are you close?" Emma called, stumbling through the door.

"Oh, Emma. Let me help you." Harriet's shoes echoed on the hardwood as she came over. Emma released her death grip on the things in her left hand as Harriet pulled them away.

"Thank you."

"You could have made two trips, you know." Harriet was used to Emma bringing her work home by now and took the bags she'd relieved Emma of and walked to Emma's room with them, laying them on the bed.

They walked back to Granddad sitting in the kitchen with his afternoon snack. Except for his end of the table, the rest of it was covered with knit hats, some lumpier than others.

"Wow, you've been busy," Emma said, coming around to give Granddad a squeeze.

"Yes, well…" Harriet gathered them all up and stuffed them in the tote bag where she stored all her yarn. She let out a long sigh filled with so much melancholy she could give Granddad a run for his money on his worst day.

"We should talk," Emma suggested. "Come to my room while I hang things up in my closet."

Emma, for all her work in fashion, did not own gobs of

clothes. She made sure everything she owned was in good condition, fit well, and was easy to pair with other things. Which left her with plenty of closet space for storing client items. Sometimes it was a bigger hassle to return something than to keep it, and if the item was a good enough find, she'd save it for a future client.

Harriet sat on the floor with her back to Emma's bed. "I broke things off with Martin today."

"You did?" Emma froze, feeling both awful and elated at the same time. She grabbed a stack of skirts off the bed and hid in the closet with her mixed emotions. "I'm so sorry, Harriet. I feel responsible."

"Oh, no. You can't blame yourself. You've been nothing but nice to me." Harriet blew her nose. "It's just ... I don't know what to do without him."

"But maybe that's a sign it wasn't a very balanced relationship, Harriet. Maybe you need someone independent, where you can each do your own thing while being together, something a little less intense."

A glance back told her Harriet was considering this, her face in deep thought while her fingers plucked at the carpeting.

"There is absolutely no pressure, but there's someone I want you to meet at this dinner party. I think you two would balance each other nicely. You have all the qualities he's looking for, and I've known him a long time. He's a good guy."

Harriet shook her head. "Oh, I don't know. It's way too soon to be thinking about that."

"But that's the great part about this. You don't have to jump into anything serious. You've done serious. Too serious. Maybe casually dating someone will help you figure out what you want."

"That makes sense, I guess." Harriet looked up, suddenly alarmed. "You haven't told this guy about me, have you?"

Emma firmly shook her head, so glad she could answer with 100% honesty. "Of course not. He has no idea I'm even interested in setting him up."

With everything hung up in the closet, Emma turned and put a hand out to help Harriet off the floor. "Everything will be okay, I promise."

Harriet took the boost off the floor and the boost to her doldrums. "It is going to be okay, isn't it? My mama always said, 'The bright side has better lighting.'"

"She sounds wise. You should call her."

Harriet looked wistful. "We haven't talked in a while. It's been so long I don't think a simple, 'I'm sorry' would cut it."

Emma was fond of giving advice, maybe too fond of it. George sure seemed to think so, but even he would tell her to speak up now. "My mom died when I was four. Call your mother."

"Yes, ma'am." Harriet gathered her coat and purse from the entryway. "Thank you, Emma."

***

George glanced at the incoming call from Emma and sighed. He had just chosen a stool by the window of his favorite Mexican food place and his foil-wrapped burrito lay in all its glory on the red tray in front of him.

Emma knew his schedule too well. If she'd planned to call him, did this mean she wanted to talk about their relationship possibly changing? That was something he'd rather do in person when he wasn't hungry, or irritable, and he didn't have his mind in work mode.

Before it could go to voicemail, he answered the call. "Yes?"

"You don't have to sound so put out, George. Is this a bad time?" Leave it to Emma to go straight into a lecture.

"No. I just want to eat my lunch while it's warm, and I don't want to talk with my mouth full. You're making me choose."

"Go ahead and talk with your mouth full. I'm not sitting across from you. Oh, is someone sitting across from you?"

"No." Only a greedy-looking pigeon patrolling the window sill. George rapped on the window, and it clumsily flew away.

"Well, good. It's about the dinner party."

Of course, it was. Relief warred with pre-boredom. If he

had to hear about feather boas and the salad course one more time…

"I need you to ask your receptionist Jane to come, and see if she can bring a date, like that friend of hers you met."

"Emma, I just got through telling her she'd need to stay with her grandmother so Betty could go."

"Rats. It's just, Isabella called me, and she came down with a bad cold. She's not sure she'll be well enough to go, and John won't come without her."

Well, there went George's chance of having a good time at this thing. George took a quick bite while he thought. "Emma, if I have to ask Jane, and make sure one of their neighbors can look in on her grandmother that night, I want some answers about why you're even having this party. And don't tell me because it's fun. This is work. This is 'sometimes romance needs a little nudge.' Are you trying to set up Elton and Harriet? I was thinking about everyone else who's going, and those two stick out as high suspects."

George got another three bites in while Emma was silent on the other end. It was as bad as he'd feared. It had only been a hunch until now.

"Okay, it is for Elton, but I'm not necessarily setting him up with Harriet. I invited Nicole and Cara, too."

George tried not to growl. "Nicole and Cara would not be interested in Elton, and you know it. They like jocks and businessmen who used to be jocks."

Emma sighed. "Darn, that's actually true. What about Jane? Do you think she'd be Elton's type?"

George let go of a little bit of his worries. Emma was like an overzealous matchmaking mother seeking grandchildren. She should find Elton's mother and team up with her. Maybe if they successfully married him off, he'd stop coming over to Emma's house at night.

"It's possible they'd hit it off, but unlikely. Look, if I ask Jane, and Isabella has a miraculous recovery, will I have to tell Jane she's not coming? Because I'm not doing that. I still have to work with her."

"No way. We'd buy the kit add-ons if that happens. I'd

rather have more than I expect than less. Invite her."

"Okay, okay. Now let me get back to this burrito."

Emma laughed. "Eat in peace, dear."

CHAPTER 10 ♥ TOMMY TWO FINGERS

"I'm so nervous about tonight." Emma stood behind Harriet's chair and surveyed the perfect flapper-style curls in Harriet's hair. "Okay, it's time for the headband."

Harriet picked up the feathered and jeweled headpiece from the counter and handed it to Emma. "You can't be nearly as nervous as I am." Harriet turned her head from side to side. "This is amazing. I wish Martin could see me like this." She looked up at Emma. "Sorry. I'm trying to move on, but it's hard not to think of him at times. I still think of him pretty much all the time."

"I understand." Though Emma wasn't sure she did. What would it be like to love someone so much they were a part of everything you did? The question sent a little flashback into her mind of sitting on the couch with George, asking a similar question and seeing a recognition in his eyes that things between them were changing. She shivered at the memory. Was love like that?

The doorbell rang, and Emma jumped. "That better be the caterer and not a guest."

She and Harriet clattered down the hall in their heels, and Harriet held the door open while Emma directed the man from the restaurant to bring all the trays into the kitchen.

Granddad shuffled in, wearing the pinstriped suit and black

fedora she'd picked out for him. With the slightly grumpy look he always had, he looked like the formidable mobster he'd be playing. Granddad pulled back a foil wrapper to peek inside. "Ooh, shrimp."

Emma was about to shoo him away so she and Harriet could get to work, but stopped short. Thanks to Harriet's gentle mentoring, Granddad was now used to helping out in the kitchen.

"Granddad, if I get you a serving bowl, could you fill it up with these rolls and cover it with a towel?"

He nodded and automatically moved to the linen drawer, pulling out a kitchen towel.

Emma almost got teary watching him, thinking of how much better things were with Harriet here, but spoiling her dramatic makeup would definitely put her behind schedule, and there was too much to be done.

Carefully maneuvering an apron over her side chignon and beaded headpiece, Emma tied it on and made sure it covered all of her gold tasseled gown.

She hurried to get down a serving bowl and tongs, going over in her mind all the roles of all her guests. It wouldn't do to break character by forgetting details and having to check the script. Harriet, as Kitty Darling, was supposed to flirt with every man in sight. Seating her next to Elton, aka, Mayor Graft, ensured the two would have plenty of opportunities to get to know each other.

When the doorbell rang with the first guest, Emma rushed Granddad and Harriet to their seats in the dining room and forced herself to slow as she approached the door. At the last minute, she remembered her apron and carefully removed it before shoving it in the drawer of the shoe storage bench.

It was time to be Margaret O'Hara, owner of The Dancing Bear, the hottest Speak Easy in town. Of course, the alcohol was as fake as her name. She'd promised Granddad there would be no real drinking when she'd talked him into taking part. Instead, she had sparkling cider in every flavor imaginable.

Nicole squealed when Emma opened the door and they saw each other. Her roommate from college had moved a few hours away, but Emma knew she'd be all in on something like this.

"Emma, you look absolutely dahh-ling!"

Emma put a finger to her lips. "It's Margaret O'Hara, ma'am. Do you have the password to enter?"

"Oh, yes." Nicole glanced down at her invitation. "As the crow flies."

"Come on in. And you are?"

Nicole did a little curtsey in her flapper dress. "I am Ginger Valentine."

The name suited her perfectly, as Nicole had naturally gorgeous red hair and she'd pinned it up with heart gems.

"Welcome, Ginger. Here are the rules of my establishment. You'd do well to look them over." Emma handed her the script for Ginger's character and hid a smile. George, twirly mustache and all, was coming up the walk, with an older woman on his arm. She was wearing a bright pink Mumu and bunny slippers.

It took all of Emma's concentration to stay in character. "May I help you two?"

George took off his fedora and placed it against his chest. "Ma'am, I happened to be in the neighborhood and ran into this nice neighbor lady of yours. I'm afraid she's very confused. She seems to think she lives next to an underground bar, but I assured her that's not the case. This is the laundry place, isn't it?"

"Did you need your laundry done?" Emma asked.

"As the crow flies, yes I do." George winked at her. He was much better at this acting stuff than he'd let on.

"And what is your name, sir?"

"Mr. Peabody. And this lady right here is ...." he waited for Betty to fill in the blank, but she looked terrified.

Emma gave her an encouraging smile.

Betty twisted her fingers together. "I'm Agatha Blume."

Agatha was now supposed to insist on coming inside or she would call the police, but as it was all she could do to squeak out her name, George insisted for her, and the two of them entered. Emma handed them their scripts so they could read their full backstories and know what they were supposed to keep secret about themselves and what they could share while mingling.

"How are you, George?" Granddad asked, and then quickly recovering, moved into his New York accent. "Have we met, young man? I neva forgetta face."

Emma and George exchanged knowing smiles. Granddad, not wanting to commit to something he didn't understand, had studied his character with Harriet all week.

Emma put her arms around the two men. "Mr. Peabody, I'd like you to meet Tommy Two Fingers."

George shook granddad's hand as if they'd never met before. "Tommy Two Fingers, huh? How'd you get a name like that?"

Granddad narrowed his eyes. "Because when I do this—" He snapped his fingers. "I get whatever I want."

Emma covered her mouth and turned away to hide her laugh. Granddad's delivery of that line still made her giggle every time. She'd been hesitant to give him the part, but once she realized letting Granddad be the murder victim would allow him to go off to bed early, the decision made itself.

After topping off everyone's 'drinks,' at the table, Emma headed back to the front door just in time to greet Elton striding up in his three-piece suit with a gaudy pocket watch on a chain.

"Mayor Graft, how nice of you to come."

Elton gave her a quick kiss on the cheek. "I've been looking forward to this."

"Excellent. Let me show you where you'll be sitting." Emma had place cards, but she didn't want to take any chances. She had to ensure Elton and Harriet sat together and were properly introduced.

With a raised eyebrow and a sly point at Elton's back, Emma alerted Harriet of his arrival, and Harriet stopped fiddling with her flute of cran-apple cider and turned toward them.

"Mayor Graft, this is Kitty Darling. Perhaps you've heard of her. She's a very famous singer."

Elton took Harriet's hand and kissed the back of it. "Longtime fan, Miss Kitty."

Emma had goosebumps. Chemistry galore was going on between those two already. "I'll just leave you two to chat."

She turned with a smile and all but ran into George, who looked suspicious and poised to give her a piece of his mind. If she could put it off until after the party, this would all be worth it. Elton and Harriet would both be happy, and George would see he was worrying for nothing.

"Excuse me." She darted around him, and as if fate had decided to help her out, the doorbell rang, giving her an excuse to flee the dining room again.

This time it was George's friends, Jane and Finn. Jane wasn't wearing much of a costume, though she was certainly striking in a nice pair of jeans and a flowy blouse with a long string of pearls. George hadn't mentioned what she looked like, and Emma couldn't help a small twinge of jealousy, as ridiculous as it was. Afraid Jane would somehow sense her thoughts, Emma made sure to give them both an extra friendly welcome. Jane's returning smile was as wooden as a brand new Pinocchio. She stood silently by while Finn, decked out like a Prohibition-era gangster, gave the password and a wink.

That was a little odd. George had said how nice Jane was in the office. Maybe something had happened on their way here— a fight or something. Emma knew they were old friends, but nothing else about these two.

"Your costume is amazing," Finn whispered to her as they passed to come inside. He gave her a backward glance before he and Jane turned to enter the dining room—a look that could only be described as *interested*.

Finn was certainly handsome, but as an unknown entity who was only visiting from out of town, there was no way Emma would take his flirting seriously. Still, it was a little flattering. This night was full of all sorts of interesting surprises.

***

George reminded himself that his main objective in coming was to make sure Betty had a good time, and he couldn't do that if he continued to brood. Betty needed all the help she could get. He'd never seen her at a loss for words before, but somehow acting was her kryptonite. Every time someone would talk to her, she'd bury her face in her script and hesitatingly read off the same line about herself—"I live next door, and if I had it my way, this whole place would be shut down."

He caught Emma rolling her eyes the fourth time Betty said it, and he could have sworn steam came out of his ears. If he didn't love Emma so much he'd absolutely hate her right now.

Her hosting skills took a dive the moment she'd introduced Elton and Harriet to each other and only got worse when Finn and Jane arrived. When she wasn't blatantly staring at Elton and Harriet, trying to listen in on their conversation, Emma was blushing under Finn's attention to her. And why was he paying her so much attention?

Finn had arrived with slicked-back hair he continued to tame with a comb from his shirt pocket, fully throwing himself into the part of Dr. Archibald, the town doctor with questionable credentials. He was friendly with everyone, snapping his red suspenders and winking back at Jane while he talked to Emma's old college friends, Nicole and Cara. Jane ignored him.

Whatever Finn's reasons for punishing her, it wasn't right. There was no excuse to leave Jane out and rub his flirting in her face, whether they were 'just friends' or not. George began to rethink everything he'd initially assumed about those two.

He glanced at his script. Until the murder occurred, there was nothing to do but finish eating and try not to watch Emma. Finn was sitting to her right, and all through dinner he'd been leaning into her, whispering things and making her laugh. How could she not care that Jane was right there, on his other side?

Emma did look amazing in her flapper dress. There was no denying it. The tassels swinging back and forth were meant to draw the eye, but that didn't give Finn the right to look on in appreciation every time she moved around the table to check on things. He was too obvious about it.

"George, the script says I should mention my son, Mugsy. I guess he's a gangster or something. Who should I tell?" Betty looked around and then back down at her paper.

"Why don't you practice on me," George offered. He needed to be more like Jane, indifferent to everything, though if

77

he got the chance tonight, he'd subtly hint to Jane that maybe she should send Finn back to Sacramento and forget about him. There was such a thing as being too indifferent.

"Have I told you about my son, Mugsy?" Betty asked.

"Mugsy? Never heard of him. Look, lady. The less I know about you the better. Aren't you planning to rat me out for being at a fine establishment like this?"

Betty's eyes widened. "Well, maybe not you, Mr. Peabody."

"Good job," George whispered. "You've got this."

Betty blushed. "I think I am starting to get the hang of this." She turned to her right and initiated a hesitant conversation with Austin, who looked about as excited to be there as Jane. He'd been under the assumption this party would include a lot of alcohol. Unlike George, he'd already had it out with Emma for deceiving him into coming. Their college friendship had been based on Austin's interest in dating Emma's friends. Why they were still friends, George wasn't sure.

At least Austin was being nice to Betty. They went back and forth with the script, taking turns revealing things about their characters.

Emma stood and tapped a spoon against her glass and everyone quieted. George recognized this as his cue to go shut off the lights so Mr. Woodhouse could be murdered. A stubborn part of George wanted to stay seated, but Mr. Woodhouse was already looking tired and ready to go off to bed, and the uncertain pleading in Emma's expression had George pushing back his chair and moving to the wall to comply.

"A toast," Emma said. "To good times, and good friends."

George shut off the lights, and there were several gasps and one scream he recognized as Emma's. Two more seconds and he flipped the lights back on.

Mr. Woodhouse gave an Oscar-worthy performance of a dead guy slumped in his chair. A silver dagger was tucked in his armpit.

Emma gasped. "Tommy Two Fingers is dead, and someone here killed him!"

There was a rustle of papers as everyone consulted their

scripts for what to do next.

Finn stood up and rounded the table. "I'm the doctor. Let me have a look-see. Maybe he's not dead."

He lifted Mr. Woodhouse's arm, the one not cradling a knife, and let it drop back down. "He's dead all right."

It was Betty's turn, and George gave her a slight nudge and pointed to the script.

"Oh." Betty adjusted her glasses and squinted at the page. "Dr. Archibald. Get your hands off that body. You're tamping with evidence."

"I'm tampering," Finn corrected. He and Emma glanced at each other, hiding little amused smiles.

Who did this guy think he was? George stood. "Agatha is right. Stop touching the body, and let's call the police." He'd stolen Nicole's line, but she was having a whispered conversation with Cara, and he wanted to move the attention away from Betty's mistake. He'd have to make sure Betty went to the optometrist soon and got a new eye prescription.

Emma stared him down, the first time she'd made meaningful eye contact with him since putting Harriet and Elton next to each other, which only confirmed his suspicion that her matchmaking scheme for those two was way deeper than she'd let on. "No one is calling the police. We'd all be arrested and this place would be shut down. No, I say we find the murderer ourselves and let Mayor Graft deal with him. What say you, Mayor?"

Elton, looking self-important, as any corrupt mayor should, nodded his agreement. "We have ways of taking care of these things. Don't you worry, Margaret O'Hara."

Granddad groaned and stretched. "That's about all my back can take." He deposited the knife on the table and yawned. "I want all of you out of here by nine."

Emma laughed. "Or close to that. Come on, Two Fingers." She moved to his chair at the same time Harriet came around to help him.

"Let me, Emma. I don't know the script as well and it doesn't matter if I hear all the clues."

Emma gave a small shake of her head. "We'll be fine. You

79

should stay and keep an eye on that mayor. Maybe *he's* the murderer."

Harriet glanced at Elton. "Oh, I … uh… Well, okay."

That reluctant submission in Harriet's face was the last straw. The knot forming in George's chest gave a mighty squeeze, and he carefully excused himself and followed Emma and Mr. Woodhouse down the hall.

Even watching her sweetly chat with Mr. Woodhouse while she helped him take his shoes off didn't loosen that knot. He waited in the doorway, and Emma glanced his way, looking resigned.

She shut Mr. Woodhouse's door and met him in the dark hallway.

"Just say it, George," she whispered.

"Say what? What am I going to say?"

"Everyone has their complaints. I get it. Austin wanted booze. Nicole was hoping I'd invite more single guys. You want me to not use this perfect opportunity for matchmaking. Am I right?"

"Emma, this is not a joke. Your understanding of what I want is only skimming the surface of why you're wrong about this."

Her mouth dropped open slightly. "Chill out. I'm not making arranged marriages here. I used place setting cards to put two people next to each other. That's not a crime."

"Harriet has a boyfriend, and you are her boss. You're putting her in an uncomfortable position by including her in your matchmaking. Trying to please you should not include dating the person you assign her. Can't you see that?"

Emma glanced away. "Harriet broke up with her boyfriend."

"And why is that?" George put his hand on her arm to get her attention and quickly let it go. Just that small touch was a distraction he didn't need.

"I didn't tell her to break up with him!"

"I bet you didn't have to. Harriet looks up to you, she listens. I don't think it was a secret you didn't like Martin. That kind of power is dangerous. Sometimes, Emma, you just don't read people well."

"I don't read people well? What does that even mean?"

"For one, stop flirting with Finn. He's using you to get back at Jane."

"I'm not flirting with him. He's flirting with me. And I just met these people, so how would I just magically know his motives? *You* tell him to stop flirting with me."

Actually, those were good points. He shouldn't have brought up Finn. It made him sound jealous, which he was mostly not. "If I say something, he'll assume it's because I have some claim on you."

Emma's dark blue eyes studied him intently, and his breathing picked up. "And you've made no such claim." Her gaze dropped to his lips before flitting back up.

But they weren't done talking, and he owed it to Harriet to make Emma understand.

"I get why you want Elton for Harriet. He's a neighbor, and he'll never get serious with her. That's convenient for you, of course. But it's not your place to rearrange her love life for your own comfort. Love is complicated, Emma. It's not meant for the boxes you try to stuff it in. You can't just flip a switch and fix things. Elton is no Band-Aid, and certainly, no replacement for the close relationship Harriet shared with her boyfriend."

Emma's jaw tightened. "She wasn't happy with Martin, and I've given this a lot of thought. Elton and Harriet make sense together. Maybe you're the one who's wrong. Have you ever considered that?"

"I'm not wrong, and you'll come to see it."

She crossed her arms and glared back at him. "Go back to your date, already. Betty's waiting for you to help her with her lines."

"Oh, very mature, Emma. You're the one who called me up all frantic when your sister got sick."

"Well, next time come up with better replacements," Emma hissed. She moved to stomp away and froze.

Someone must have overheard them. George glanced back and wished he could rewind time. It was like the icing on this dump cake of an evening.

Betty stood at the end of the hallway with downcast eyes, hugging her middle. "They sent me to fetch you two."

Emma fled around her, leaving George to fix this. He put his arm around Betty to lead her back into the dining room. Her bunny slippers swooshed against the carpet, reminding him how out of her element she must feel.

"I told you I shouldn't have come," she whispered.

"We had a fight. This has nothing to do with you, Betty." George let out a frustrated breath, grasping for the right words. "I wanted this to be a fun night for you. That's the only reason I invited you. Jane and Finn were the last minute replacements. And although I'm really disappointed in Emma, she's a good person at heart. It's just buried down deep right now."

CHAPTER 11 ♥ YOU CAN ALL GO HOME

George couldn't be right about this. He just couldn't be. Except now, every time Finn made eye contact and gave Emma one of his secret smiles or little compliments, she longed to punch him in the nose. The flattery she'd felt previously was now a big embarrassment, proof she was as shallow and self-serving as George had branded her.

Throwing herself into her role as host, she served dessert while plowing through the script, cringing each time it was Betty's turn, and she botched it. Betty threw her apologetic glances every time. It was more evidence of Emma's pettiness, caught making fun of an old woman trying her best.

At least Elton and Harriet were hitting it off. Elton's arm was around the back of Harriet's chair, and he'd tasted a bite of her chocolate cheesecake to see if it was as good as his raspberry slice. That had to mean something, right? If this night worked out for them, it would all be worth it.

A few more clues and accusations and everyone would go home. Elton would walk Harriet out to her car. Emma could rest her aching head and clean up in the morning.

It was her turn in the script. "Dr. Archibald, isn't it true you and Tommy Two Fingers used to play poker together?"

Finn leaned in, too close for comfort, and in a low voice said, "What's it to you?"

Emma recoiled from him. He really was a worm, or a good

actor. At this point, she didn't care which. "You owed him a lot of money."

Finn pointed across the table. "So did Mr. Peabody. And now neither of us have to pay up. I'd say it's our lucky night."

Betty's turn. Emma kept a neutral face and poked at her dessert. Betty seemed to do worse when she knew people were looking at her.

"Well, I had no cause to kill him. I shouldn't even be here."

Yes! Emma almost clapped at the perfectly executed line, but as it was time to accuse Betty of murder, Emma put on a stern face instead. "Oh, you had cause as well, Agatha. Your son, Mugsy, used to come in here with Tommy Two Fingers, but one night they had a row, and Mugsy ain't been seen since."

"Yeah, where's Mugsy?" George demanded.

"Well, I don't know. Let me see what my script says about him." Betty wrinkled her forehead as she frantically flipped through pages. At least she missed the eye rolls from Nicole and Cara.

"Would anyone like more dessert?" Emma asked, trying to fill the lull. They all shook their heads or ignored the question. Nobody wanted anything. Cara was not-so-stealthily trying to scratch under her wig, and Jane, aloof as ever, continued to absently slide her finger down her phone, clearly bored with whatever she was looking at, but not willing to give it up if the alternative meant paying attention to the murder mystery game. Time to end this thing.

"Oh, it says here Mugsy's in the slammer and Tommy put him there," Betty said, looking pleased with herself.

"Sounds like a motive to me. Agatha, did you kill Tommy Two Fingers out of revenge?"

"I hope not."

That was as good of improv as they'd get out of her. Emma passed out slips of papers and pencils to everyone. "Now that you've heard all the evidence, write your guesses. Then we'll see if anyone would like to confess." *So you can all go home.* There had to be easier ways to get two people together. Emma enjoyed helping people, one fashion disaster at a time. Party planning was a whole different animal—a balancing act of blending personalities and needs. She wouldn't try it again any time soon.

There were three guesses for Agatha, three for Dr. Archibald, two for Mayor Graft, and one for Ginger. Nobody guessed the real killer, Margaret O'Hara, their host. Emma read her confession which included her attempt to frame Agatha, thanked everyone for coming, and then took aside Elton to ask him if he could make sure Harriet made it safely to her car. George's glare was like a laser beam pointed at her forehead, but what did it matter now? He didn't like the matchmaking. Message received loud and clear. She was feeling a little detached from it all at the moment.

Finn offered to stay and help clean up, and since he and Jane rode together, that meant he was offering on Jane's behalf as well. Emma kindly but firmly turned him down and actually got a half-smile out of Jane.

She thought she had everyone out when she strode into the kitchen and slammed a cupboard shut.

"Can I do that too?"

Emma jumped. She wasn't alone yet. "Go away, George. I don't like you right now."

"Come on, Emma. Can't we talk about this?" He sighed the way a parent might when dealing with a moody teenager.

It certainly didn't improve her mood. "I'm not sorry for trying to set up Harriet and Elton, so if you're looking for an apology, I don't have one to give you."

"I don't think either of us is in the mood to swap apologies. I was as much an idiot tonight as you. Poor Betty got the brunt of that." He took off his fedora and mangled it in his hands. "But you were very careful in what you said about your matchmaking with Elton, and when I asked you if this party was a setup for Elton and Harriet, you pretty much lied about that, too. I'm not used to you being evasive and prickly with me. I'm not sure why we can't just talk about this like real friends, but I'm done trying for tonight. I'm really disappointed Emma. I thought I knew you better than that." He gave her one last penetrating look and walked out.

She didn't follow him to the door. His words stung, and she had no defense from what he'd said. Once she was sure he was gone, she walked over and locked the front door. The sign she'd had specially printed for the party was sitting on an easel and she picked it up and ripped it in half—a long, slow rip that was especially satisfying.

And then she cried. Emma never cried. But she couldn't get the tears to stop. She went into the den where she and George always watched TV together and turned on an episode of *Princess Wars*, still crying.

CHAPTER 12 ♥ HER PHONE BOYFRIEND WAS NICER

George pulled into his parking spot in front of his apartment and sat there, mulling things over. He should have taken Betty home, but she'd left with Jane and Finn. He hadn't finished saying all the things he wanted to say to Emma, but lecturing her more hadn't made him feel better. In fact, he felt much, much worse. He didn't want to go inside and sit in front of the TV. Sleep was out of the question.

What he needed was a plan, a goal. Going inside and changing into gym clothes, he got back in his car and drove to the 24-hour gym around the corner. He didn't belong to this one. It was small and smelled too strongly of disinfectant, but he paid for a daily pass and picked out a stair climber.

He felt better with every passing minute and each simulated flight of stairs. Somehow, his life had incrementally intertwined closer and closer with Emma's. Maybe it was time to dial that back and focus on other things. It couldn't be that hard, could it?

His phone rang, and he pulled it out warily, afraid of who might be calling this late. But it was Jane. What could she want?

"Jane? Is everything okay with your aunt and grandmother?"

"Yes, everything is fine. It's just … will you tell Emma I'm sorry?"

"Of course." He slowed his pace so he could hear her better.

"I shouldn't have even come tonight in the mood I was in."

George waited, but she didn't elaborate. "It was nice of you to agree to it last minute," he finally said.

"I'm embarrassed about the way I acted, and about the way … well, anyway, I'm just sorry you had to see me like that."

"It's okay, Jane. We're coworkers, and maybe it's best if we just stick with that, despite your aunt's worries for your social life."

"Yes. Let's!" Her relief was palpable, and he was glad he hadn't offended her, and she'd understood what he meant. He felt like they were both talking around what was really going on. Jane wasn't just apologizing for herself. It was Finn's behavior, not just hers, requiring an apology, though she hadn't once mentioned his name.

"So, I'll see you Monday?" he asked.

"Monday." Jane said goodbye, and he put his phone away, ramping up his speed so he could finish the programmed workout.

That was one relationship in his life he had successfully put back into order, which gave him hope for one a lot more important. And Emma was important to him. Why else would he care so much what she did? His disappointment in her ate at him. He felt guilty for wanting her to be the person he knew she could, and guilty that he'd let jealousy cloud his judgment tonight. That flapper dress had really been something else. He shook his head to clear the image and kept climbing.

***

Emma dragged her phone toward her and waited for her bleary eyes to focus so she could shut off the alarm.

The sting of George's words hadn't quite subsided yet, though she tried to push them away. There was no wrong he didn't want to right. Maybe it was the caregiver in him. Harriet wasn't even aware of his concern, yet he felt it all the same. Of course, anyone who met Harriet immediately loved her. She had that kind of magnetism.

Emma cared about Harriet too, despite what George thought. Emma wasn't the selfish manipulator he thought she was. Last night was for Harriet's benefit, and the alarm that had just gone off was for Harriet's benefit, too. The house was a disaster, and Emma wouldn't leave it for Harriet to clean up, even if it was part of her job. There would be other Saturdays to sleep in.

Emma's neck and back protested as she dragged herself out of bed, but she got ready anyway with her normal efficiency. She only had two hours before she needed to leave for an appointment with a new client, a single mom who suddenly needed a professional wardrobe by Monday after a lifetime of jeans and sweats. Finding expensive-looking pieces that were not expensive took strategy. Every item they bought would need to work in multiple outfit combinations. The clothes would also need to be sturdy, with at least one outfit that wouldn't have to be dry cleaned or pressed. Emma relished the challenge. Having things to do meant she didn't have to dwell on yesterday's disasters.

With hands on her hips, Emma surveyed the dining room. The 'murder weapon' was still sitting on Granddad's chair. Empty bottles of sparkling cider littered the table. Best to start with the heaviest things first. Dumping everything from the table onto one end, she wiped down the middle section and put away the table leaf. Extra dining chairs went into the garage. The bottles went in the recycle bin.

Harriet came in while Emma was tackling the dishes.

"Was last night too terrible?" Emma asked, gauging Harriet's face.

Harriet's responding smile was genuine. "I had a great time. Elton was just spot on as the mayor, and we had a chance to talk about so many things."

Wow, she'd brought up Elton without even being prompted. Emma couldn't help the excitement building within. "Would you want him to call you? Hypothetically speaking, of course."

Harriet shrugged. "Well, I wouldn't say no to a date." She smiled and picked up a drying towel. "But don't you be telling him that now, you hear?"

89

Emma raised her soapy hands in surrender. "I have not said a word to him. However, I could maybe text him this week and ask if he can return the gardening shears he borrowed. You'll be home, you two could chat at the door…"

Harriet giggled. "Okay, deal. I think that's subtle enough. I took your advice and finally called Mama, and I told her all about Martin, and you, and Granddad, and Elton. She thinks I should stay and build my life here."

"It sounds like wise advice." Emma checked the time and quickly dried off her hands. "I have to go. Don't feel like you need to finish all this up. Just enjoy your day with Granddad."

He came shuffling into the kitchen right on cue. "Quite the racket you were making in here, Emma. You could wake the dead."

Emma took off her apron and kissed his cheek. "Good morning to you, too. I'll see you this afternoon."

She left the house with a much lighter heart. Things were moving slowly but promisingly between Harriet and Elton, as they should be. All that worry on George's part was for nothing. She couldn't even tell him, because that would be gloating, and he'd probably lecture her for that as well.

***

Jane and Lois were staying late at the office to cross-train on billing, and George was happy to leave a little early and let Dr. Perry referee that. It gave him an opportunity to stop in and check on Betty and Mrs. Bates without breaching the coworker-only agreement he and Jane had tentatively worked out.

Mainly, he wanted to make sure he and Emma hadn't damaged Betty's self-confidence with their stupid fight. Someone with so little to her name didn't deserve to lose her cheerful outlook on life, too.

Betty answered the door right away. "Oh, George. I'm glad I caught you. Jane and I tried our hand at baking yesterday and we're just overflowing with pumpkin bread. Do you like pumpkin things?"

"I love pumpkin."

Betty ushered him inside and over to their little kitchen counter, all the while talking about roasted pumpkin seeds, and her baking adventures, and how the grocery store was selling cans of pumpkin for seventy-five cents.

"Seventy-five cents!" Betty threw her hands into the air. "Can you imagine that? It's like they're giving it away."

George stealthily turned a can around and checked the date on it. Giving it away, indeed. But all was well for another six months. He almost hated to bring up Emma's dinner since Betty was completely distracted with happy thoughts of pumpkin sales. "So, you got home okay after the party?"

"Of course. I had a feeling you and Emma had some things to work out, and without an interfering audience like myself." She looked ashamed, as if it was her fault she'd overheard them.

"You weren't interfering, you were trying to herd us back to the party, where we should have been." He tapped the Formica countertop. "There were a lot of things wrong with that night, and none of them were your fault."

"I'm not used to all these young people and their dramas. Everywhere I turn someone's fighting or kissing, or both. I thought that only happened in soap operas."

"Kissing?" Was she referring to the party? Did she think he and Emma... or was she referring to someone else?

Betty raised an eyebrow. "I went to check on Jane before I went to bed that night. She and Finn stayed up late talking on the porch, and I walked out on them in full embrace. You won't tell her I said anything, will you?"

"Of course not." George wished he hadn't asked her to elaborate. Was that before or after Jane had called to apologize? No, it was better not to know.

"She was so embarrassed, though I'm not sure why. It's not like I've never seen kissing before. I mean, Jane and I watch that show *Cooking with Strangers* together. It's amazing they get any cooking done with all the romance and nonsense."

George laughed. "Emma likes that show, too."

"It's a bit fluffy, but it's entertainment."

Betty didn't need to play a character, she was quite the character all by herself.

He looked in on Mrs. Bates, who opened her eyes and chatted with him for a few minutes before dozing off again.

Taking his pumpkin bread gift, he said goodbye to Betty and went home.

TV was boring all by himself, but the noise was better than nothing. He checked on his fish tank, watching the snails ooze down the glass sides and wander along the gravel bed with their funny little antennae out.

He missed Emma, but he reminded himself they needed space from each other. Right now, though, space just felt like a gaping hole waiting to be filled with something.

***

Harriet met Emma at the door with a squeak and motioned for her to hurry in. "You'll never guess who came over today!"

"Um, Justin Bieber?" Emma had never seen Harriet this excited before and couldn't fathom what could have caused it. Her feet felt like buckets of cement after walking from store to store in these demon heels. Emma pulled them off one at a time and moaned at the foot freedom. All the while, Harriet bounced around her.

"No, silly. Elton. He had lunch with us, and then we talked for an hour about … well, about everything! You're right, Emma. It's so refreshing to discover new things about myself and to find someone new to talk to. Elton's amazing. He knows so much about the world, and when he smiles, I just— eek! I can't help smiling, too."

"Wow." Emma was a little taken aback by Harriet's enthusiasm, but it was contagious, and soon Emma was squealing along with her. She had Harriet replay their whole conversation so she could mine it for clues as to how Elton felt.

Granddad waved a dismissive hand at them both and continued with the puzzle he and Harriet had started on the dining room table.

"So, he returned the shears?" Emma asked.

"Yes, but he asked if he could borrow a rake, and I let him. I hope that's okay."

"Of course."

Granddad frowned, making a path of wrinkles across his forehead. "Harriet, did you check the shears? If he didn't wipe off the tree residue, it will ruin them. Clean tools are sharp tools."

"I'll check them," Emma reassured him. She turned back to Harriet. "What was his body language like? Did he lean into you?"

Harriet pursed her lips as she thought. "Yes, I think he did. And a couple of times he touched my hand or arm. He talks a lot with his hands." She glanced at her own hands sitting in her lap. "I've been so bummed lately. I used to talk to Martin about everything, but it's time to let that go and move on. Thank you, Emma. If it wasn't for you I'd still be wallowing in self-pity."

Emma couldn't enjoy the compliment. George's words would probably always echo in her ears when it came to Harriet, making Emma doubt her own motives and opinions. She gave those thoughts a mental push and gave Harriet a hug. "I'm happy you're happy."

Harriet twirled and gave Granddad a squeeze around the shoulders and then grabbed up her bag from the hook in the entry hallway. "I'll see you two lovelies tomorrow!"

Emma locked the door behind her and waved through the side window. Twitterpated. She finally had a definition in action for that word.

"What would you like for dinner?" Emma asked as she sat next to Granddad and examined his progress on the puzzle. He had all the edges done and was working on the flower bed below the crumbling retaining wall. Puzzles were made of entirely too many landscape scenes. If Emma ever decided to sit with a puzzle for more than a few minutes, it would have to be of something interesting, like a basketball coach giving his team a half-time pep talk, or kids trying to wash an overexcited dog.

"Harriet didn't make something?" he asked.

"She can't do that every night, Granddad. Besides, we have too many leftovers in the fridge."

"Maybe just eggs and toast then."

Emma nodded. That, she could do. Harriet had been very

encouraging, and the kitchen didn't intimidate Emma the way it used to, though she still burned things from time to time.

"I don't like Elton."

"What?" Emma had been so lost in thought she almost missed Granddad's words. "You've always liked Elton."

"I've never liked him. He talks too much."

To Granddad, everybody talked too much, so that wasn't a real reason. "He's a good neighbor."

Granddad shrugged. "I guess we could do worse. But Harriet could do better. Her phone boyfriend was nicer."

"Well, they broke up." Emma tamped down her irritation with him and tried to fit a piece of sky into the puzzle. It didn't fit, and she put it back in the pile. Granddad didn't say anything else about Harriet or Elton, and Emma was relieved. She didn't want to argue.

Granddad was entitled to his opinion, even if it didn't match hers. That's what George would say right now. It was like a tiny version of him was in her head, pointing his finger at everything wrong in there.

However, she'd been right about Elton and Harriet hitting it off, and she was right about helping Harriet see a whole new world of possibilities. All her matchmaking efforts hadn't been for nothing.

CHAPTER 13 ♥ THANKS FOR RETURING THE RAKE

It had been a week since the party, and a week since George had talked to Emma. He wasn't sure how it was conceivable to both miss someone and dread seeing them again, but Emma made a lot of impossible things possible. The more time that passed, the harder it was to know how to make things right. Should he wait for her to call him, or was she waiting for him to call her?

This was how most friendships died. The distance becomes awkward, so people add more distance, and more, until they never speak again.

However, he and Emma were connected by a brother and sister who would notice and question. More than that, George didn't want to lose their friendship altogether, even if they couldn't be anything more. It was a good thing they'd been interrupted when he'd almost kissed her. Having feelings for Emma had turned his perfectly ordered life upside down. It was time to go back to friendship, nothing more. The thought had his stomach in knots. He could do this. He had to.

Seven days was enough space, wasn't it? It seemed like enough. He took the coward's way forward and texted her as he was leaving work.

Hey

Just like the subject line of spam email, but everything he

typed after 'Hey' came out wrong, and he erased it again and again. So he just sent, 'hey.'

Hey yourself.

That was the Emma he knew. George sagged in relief.

Can I come over later?

Sure. Or you could come now.

Ok. Be there in 10.

And there it was. A new start.

He felt good about it until he pulled onto her street, and then doubt crept in. Maybe he did need more space. The truth had crept up on him in the same way his affection for Emma had. Somewhere along the way, he'd fallen in love with her, and right now he'd give anything to fall right back out. But he had promised he'd come.

After parking out front, he knocked lightly. Emma called for him to come in, so he walked inside and sat at the dining table with her and Mr. Woodhouse where they were working on a puzzle. Well, Mr. Woodhouse was working on the puzzle. Emma was studying it with the same enjoyment level as a calculus test. Somehow, that didn't surprise him.

Her eyes came up to meet George's, and he saw the same hesitation he felt, echoed in her expression. But there was nothing they had to say right now with Mr. Woodhouse in the room. George reached for a few puzzle pieces and examined the picture.

"How are things?" he finally asked.

"Fine. Are you hungry? I could make you something." She smiled self-consciously. "Or you could make yourself something. That's a safer bet."

"The eggs were good, Emma," Mr. Woodhouse said, patting her hand.

"I'm not hungry." He was, but he feared Emma following him into the kitchen where they'd be alone. This was hopeless. Mr. Woodhouse's schedule was very rigid. In twenty minutes he'd go get ready for bed and watch a little CNN. Which meant, in twenty minutes, George and Emma would be alone together regardless.

George put down the puzzle piece he'd been holding for the

past two minutes, having never put any real effort into finding the place it belonged. He looked up to see Emma studying him, her perfect lips puckering slightly.

"You two are no help when it comes to this thing," mused Mr. Woodhouse. He stole the pieces George had tried to attach and put them back in the color-coordinated piles in front of him.

"Puzzles aren't really my thing," Emma admitted.

"That's something defeatists say."

"Granddad," Emma warned. "You're being crotchety with me."

"Well, I feel crotchety. How about you, George? You seem out of sorts. Any complaints to air?"

George thought quickly. "These socks are quitters. I'm throwing these out when I get home." He pulled up his pant legs for Mr. Woodhouse to see, which led to a thorough assessment and diagnosis that indeed, the sock elastic must be bad, or possibly the material, or both.

"Anything else you two want to complain about?" Emma asked with a roll of her eyes.

"Yes," Mr. Woodhouse demanded. "Is Elton going to return that rake? He keeps coming over and talking incessantly to Harriet, but he never brings the rake like he says he will."

Emma's face turned a bright red. "I'm sure he'll bring it. Or, if it's really bothering you, tomorrow's Saturday, and I don't have any appointments. I'll go get it from him."

So the matchmaking continued. That was a little disappointing. But when did Emma ever listen to him? George scolded himself for worrying about it again. What was done was done.

And what did it matter what Emma did? He'd given his advice, his warnings, but Emma was who she was, and she had no interest in changing. Wishing for her to live up to the ideals he'd foolishly created for her would only lead to disappointment and unhappiness for both of them, more than he already felt.

***

97

George had practically bolted for the door the second Granddad declared he was heading to bed. Maybe it would be better if they waited for another day to talk, but Emma hated to leave things so strained between them. This was almost worse than not hearing from George and assuming he just needed more time.

"Wait for me," she whispered with just a touch of pleading.

George reluctantly set his car keys back on the counter and waved her off, obviously sensing her fear that the second her back turned, he'd be gone.

She went down the hall with Granddad, turning on his TV and his nightlight in the bathroom, and putting his shoes neatly in his closet.

"Not more Congressional hearings," Granddad grumbled, gesturing at the TV. "Where's a good earthquake when we need it?"

"Don't tempt fate, Granddad."

"True, true. Goodnight, my Emma."

"Goodnight." She kissed his forehead before quickly retreating and sprinting down the hall.

George was not where she'd left him, and she glanced around, afraid maybe he had actually ditched her. But no, he was pacing in the entryway with his hands in his hair. He stopped short when he realized she'd returned.

"That eager to get out of here, huh?"

The blunt honesty garnered her a small smile from him. "Sorry."

He was as handsome as ever with his hair all disheveled like that. She warily approached him and reached a hand up to tame it back down.

George practically flinched from her touch, and she dropped her hand. "I was just gonna fix—never mind."

He flattened his hair himself with both hands and stepped back. "I'm sorry I lectured you about Harriet. It's none of my business what you do. Let's just try to be friends again, okay?"

She'd never known him to be jumpy, and she didn't know what to do with this side of him. Sure, she'd irritated him to death before, and vice-versa, but they'd always been able to laugh it off.

"Okay." She stuck her hands behind her, knowing there was no returning to what they'd had before. There would be no accidental touches or snuggling on the couch. There would be no going back to … them.

A sorry was on the tip of her tongue, but she choked on it and said nothing. It was her turn to apologize, but she wasn't sorry for setting up Elton and Harriet, and she hadn't intended for Betty to overhear them arguing or for Finn to be an obnoxious flirt. Fate seemed to be laughing at her, pulling out the rug from under her to expose all her faults and comparative immaturity. All she needed from George now was a patronizing pat on the head and a dismissal.

She'd dismiss him instead. "It's fine. Just go."

George rubbed his eyes. "Yeah, that's probably best." He turned to open the door, but there was a sudden knock on it— Elton's soft knock he always used so as not to wake Granddad.

George opened the door for Elton, who was standing there holding the rake Granddad had been so concerned about.

"Don't mind me, I was just leaving." George took off past Elton without a backward glance, and Emma fixed a smile on her face and invited Elton in.

She told herself she hadn't just lost the bet of her life, with Elton as the consolation prize, but tears stung the corners of her eyes, mocking her. If George could give up on them because of her stupid matchmaking, then they were better off figuring that out now.

"Hi, Elton. Thanks for returning the rake." She took it from him and set it carefully against the wall. After he left, she'd hang it up in the garage.

Pushing thoughts of George away, she took in Elton's appearance. "You look nice."

His hair was freshly gelled, and he was wearing a new crisp shirt and pants. The cologne wafting off of him was a little intense, but a nice scent. "Did you come from an important meeting or something?"

He laughed a little self-consciously. "No, nothing like that."

"Well, come into the kitchen, and we'll find something to snack on." She led the way and dug around in the pantry.

"Chips and salsa?"

"Sure."

She put the bag of tortilla chips on the counter and went to the fridge for the salsa.

"Sit for a minute, Emma. I feel like I haven't seen you in forever. You're never home during the day anymore. You text me to come over, but then you're not here. What kind of games are those?"

Elton had a weird sense of humor. She set down the salsa and leaned her elbows on the counter. "I went back to work. That's why I hired Harriet. She's a lifesaver, and Granddad and I both love her."

"Yeah, she's great." Elton rubbed his ear.

He didn't make a move toward the chips or salsa, so Emma waited, too. The way her stomach was tensing, putting food into it wasn't a good idea anyway.

"Emma, would you like to go with me to the symphony next Saturday night? A fan of one of my books gave me tickets."

"Oh, how nice of them. I'll have to check my schedule, but I'm sure Harriet would be free that night if I'm not."

Elton got off his stool and edged around the counter until he was next to her, with their shoulders practically touching. "You really do love your grandfather's nurse. But I didn't ask Harriet, I'm asking you. The performance is at eight. I thought we could go to dinner first, make a night of it."

A chill came over her, and she froze in place while her mind raced. Was Elton…? No. She'd never thought of him that way and had assumed he felt the same about her.

Elton ran one finger down her wrist, and she jumped away from him and grabbed the bag of chips in the middle of the counter with both hands. Snacks. They just needed snacks and normal conversation. With a mighty wrench, the bag popped open, sending chips scattering all over the counter.

Emma, feeling humiliated, turned to get a bowl while Elton quietly laughed.

"You gonna be okay there?" He held up a handful of chips and deposited them in the bowl in Emma's hands.

"I'm fine, I'm just … confused."

"That makes two of us. Emma, do you think I come over because I'm interested in watching silly little reality TV shows? You know why I'm here. And I think we've reached a place in our relationship where it's time to say it out loud."

Emma put her hand up. Denial was no longer an option, no matter how much she wanted it to be. "No, I don't think we need to say anything out loud. Elton, you're my neighbor and my friend, I hope. And that's all we'll ever be."

Elton's face changed from one of calm confidence to simmering resentment. "Then you should have made that clear instead of sending me signals that you wanted more."

"What about the signals you sent Harriet? She likes you."

"Harriet?" Elton scoffed. "There were no signals. All she ever talks about is her ex, the guy she loves so much that she had to break up with him. Wait, were you trying to set me up with your help? Is that why you sat her next to me at your little party?"

"She's a registered nurse, Elton. Don't call her my help. And what's wrong with home caregiving? It's a very necessary and selfless profession."

Elton sputtered. "That's not what I meant at all. What I'm trying to say is, you can't play matchmaker with your ..." He was about to say help again but stopped himself. "You don't see a conflict of interest there? Harriet's such a people pleaser she'd date Jack the Ripper if you asked her to."

"That's not true." Emma's throat closed off. Did everyone see it except her? She felt like the room was spinning, with Elton's smug face the only thing in focus. He'd practically declared his feelings, but when that tanked, he'd found a handhold to hoist himself up with so he could look down on her again. His eyes, his smirk, his stance, they all said she was naïve and clueless, and she hated that she felt the way he saw her.

Elton crossed his arms and leaned against the counter. "Even if I was interested in Harriet like that—which I'm not—there's no way I'd be her rebound guy."

"Understood." Emma bit her lip. Elton would keep going if she let him. He could milk a two-minute conversation into twenty. He just had that gift. "Thanks for returning the rake." She gestured to the door where she'd left it, hoping he'd take the hint.

Elton's chin lifted a little. "Clearly, there's been some misunderstandings on both sides. I'll find someone else to take to the symphony. See you around, Emma." He picked up a chip from the counter and popped it in his mouth before seeing himself out.

Emma didn't get the satisfaction of slamming the door on him, but she picked up the stupid rake he left and marched to the garage with it, her heart so full of anger and embarrassment that she thought she might spontaneously combust. She put the rake on its hook just the way Granddad liked it and noticed the long-handled clippers hung up next to it. Sure enough, there was sticky residue all over the blades. Elton really was a bad neighbor.

CHAPTER 14 ♥ THERE MIGHT BE SOMEONE ELSE

"Your favorite receptionist has called in sick again." Lois scrunched her nose. "And just when I was about to upgrade her from useless to slightly less useless."

"People get sick, Lois. That's the whole reason we work here, after all." George was not about to jump to conclusions the way some cynical billing specialists might, but it also had not escaped his notice that Jane's three sick days coincided with Finn's return to Sacramento.

He hadn't asked Betty whether Jane was legitimately sick because he didn't want to put her in the uncomfortable position of choosing loyalties—by either lying to him or betraying her niece.

He handed off the paperwork Jane was supposed to be doing, and Lois snatched it from his hand.

"I love you, Lois."

She grumpily waggled her head back and forth at him. "I tolerate you better than most, George. How's that for honesty?"

"Sounds about right," he said with a smile.

His next patient was waiting for him, and he went in to see Arthur, a barrel of a man in his eighties who still enjoyed a good game of tennis every morning. In addition to his regular checkup, they always looked him over for skin cancer because of his history of it, and his love for being out in the sun.

"How are we today, Arthur?"

Arthur tugged at the gown he was wearing. "I've been better. There's a spot on the side of my forehead, and I know you're going to send me to the dermatologist, and they'll send me somewhere else. Never get old, George."

"It's a trap," they said together.

Arthur laughed. "You've heard this advice before, then?"

"My brother was talking about marriage, but that's exactly the phrase he used."

Arthur shook his head. "That's a shame. Marriage shouldn't be a trap. My Betsy was the best thing that ever happened to me."

"He was joking. His wife is the best thing that ever happened to him, and he's the first to admit it when he's in a serious mood."

"Ahh. I understand."

George tipped Arthur's bald head forward a little and examined the skin there before looking at the side of his forehead where there was, indeed, the beginnings of a new skin cancer spot.

"To the dermatologist you go. Sorry, Arthur."

Thankfully, there was nothing else wrong with him, except the dreaded news that it was time, once again, to go get a colonoscopy.

"You're just full of good news, aren't you?" Arthur teased as George handed him the forms to take with him.

"It's all part of the job," George said with a shrug.

"And we appreciate that. We really do." Arthur clapped him on the shoulder and left the office. Hopefully, Lois would be nicer to Arthur than the last patient who dared approach her desk.

George's phone began vibrating with a call, which at this time of day usually meant either John or a telemarketer.

It was John.

"George, how would you feel about taking a few vacation days and going somewhere nice? And by nice, I mean to my house to watch my kids."

"I love your kids, but even I wouldn't consider that a vacation. Are you and Isabella trying to slip away for a few days before the baby comes?"

"Boy, I wish. Isabella's been having contractions, and I'm getting worried. Mom planned to fly out a few days before the baby's due date, but she can only take a week off work so I'm not sure yet whether to have her change her flight."

"Well, in that case, I'd love a vacation with your kids."

John laughed. "Sorry, I'm just trying to be prepared. This could be a false alarm, and if I need you and Mom's not here, I'm sure you and Emma can coordinate schedules and make it work. Isabella's calling Emma as we speak."

That was not reassuring. He and Emma had watched Emmy when Johnny was born, but that was back when there were no weird feelings between them, and Emmy had been a model toddler. Johnny was a poster child for why moms were always tired.

Sharing babysitting duty meant they absolutely had to get things back to normal or at least get better at faking it. He thought about calling Emma, but like John said, this was probably worried planning that would not pan out. Isabella was only at thirty-two weeks if he was remembering correctly.

"Whatever you need, John. Just keep me posted."

"Thank you, brother."

George put his phone away and got back to work.

***

Emma flipped through a rack of white blouses and pulled out one in her client's size. "Okay, Gloria. Try this one with the skirt we found."

All the worries and shame were pushed far, far, down where only Emma could see them, and she had powered through three appointments before this one without anyone asking if she was okay, including her own sister. Maybe acting was her true calling. Emma was not okay, of course. When she got home, she'd have to explain to Harriet that Elton didn't, in fact, want to date her.

When Harriet had arrived all cheerful and ready for the day, Emma couldn't bear to tell her right then, but putting it off just meant dwelling on it some more. She'd been so wrong about so many things.

Emma wasn't used to feeling uncomfortable in her own skin or in doubting her intuition, but right now, she was pretty much questioning everything.

Emma was not a matchmaker, she was a disaster. The crawly feeling of regret ate away at her, reminding her she'd thought George was judgmental and nosing into her business. Now, he had every right to say 'I told you so.'

Gloria came out of the dressing room, and Emma quickly filed those thoughts away. Gloria was paying for Emma's time, and she deserved the best.

"What do you think?" Gloria asked, crossing and uncrossing her arms.

Emma walked around her in a semi-circle. "Hmm. It's a little see-through. And I want it to work not just as an undershirt, but on its own. Let's keep looking."

They scoured the whole store for possibilities and then walked next door. Having two quality stores in close proximity made it a prime location. They were used to Emma coming and pretty much let her have the run of the place, including her own dressing room they didn't unlock for other customers and a fifteen percent discount for all her clients. Here, she was important and needed. Boutique places like this relied on her to give them steady business.

She wished she felt as confident in everything else.

Gloria ended up with almost everything she needed, and she and Emma scheduled a follow up in two weeks. With a little time to try everything out, the client would have a much better idea of what was still lacking and what was working. Chances were good they'd end up returning one or two items that never left the closet. Clients often couldn't verbalize what it was they had against the item, but it usually was just something so outside their comfort zone they couldn't bring themselves to wear it beyond the dressing room at the store, no matter how fabulous it might look on them.

Emma rehearsed what she might say to Harriet on the drive home—different explanations and suggestions for where to go from here. She was actually feeling okay about it until she realized what she was doing: trying to solve something that was never any of her business in the first place.

Elton's, and Granddad's, and George's words went round and round in her head, and the truth sank like a stone deep inside her. What right did she have to give Harriet advice? About anything? George had said she didn't read people well, probably not even herself.

Emma rubbed a hand over her face. Self-improvement was much harder than a makeover. But that's what had to be done. A makeover from the inside. No one else could know about it. Because what if she failed? What if they watched to see if she fell back into the same old patterns? And what if she did?

She got out and went into the house where she greeted Granddad and sat down just in time to see him put the final pieces into his puzzle. Harriet came out to watch too. Apparently, he'd been working on it on and off all day.

"Don't you feel accomplished?" Harriet asked him.

"I feel like I want my kitchen table back. What happened to the bottom of the box?"

The three of them searched high and low until they found it in the recycle bin. Harriet had mistaken it for shipping packaging when she was tidying up.

Harriet grabbed up her purse, and Emma knew her window of opportunity was closing. The weak part of her wanted to put it off for tomorrow. After all, Elton hadn't even come up in the conversation today. But she knew Harriet occasionally texted back and forth with him, and that couldn't happen again. Elton couldn't be the one to tell her. He was about as subtle as a sledgehammer.

"Hey, could we talk for a minute?"

Harriet glanced up from digging in her purse. "Sure."

Granddad was reading his John Grisham novel in the other room.

Harriet set her purse down and sat in one of the front room chairs they never used. They were Granny's chairs, so Emma kept them there, in the same spot by the window. She sat in the other one and kneaded her fingers together.

"I'm not sure where to start, except that what I have to tell you needs to be all true, with nothing that tries to put me in a better light. Because the light shining on me is ugly right now."

Harriet cocked her head, looking concerned. "Miss Emma, you are worrying me a little. Is everything okay?"

"No, things are pretty much terrible." She could admit it now. There was no reason to keep it all tucked away anymore. "I questioned your relationship with Martin and planted seeds of doubt in your mind, and I lied to myself about my intentions, telling myself it was for your good. But the whole time I was worried you would quit and move to be with him, and I was happy when you broke up. I thought if I could just find you a boyfriend here, it wouldn't matter. But Elton was a bad choice. He's not right for you, and you're not right for him. In fact, last night he came over and asked *me* out. I've been contacting him, asking him personal questions, all in a quest to set him up with you, and he thought it meant I was interested in him."

Harriet cleared her throat. "Well, when it rains, it pours." She blew out a long breath. "Oh, dear."

"It's okay to be mad at me. I would be."

"I'm a little mad. And a little bit not sure what to do now."

Emma resisted the urge to tell her what to do. She couldn't fix this for Harriet, and she shouldn't. The fact that advice just automatically populated inside Emma's head was a good indication that this habit might take a while to break.

Harriet shook her head. "So, Elton, he … are you two together now?"

"No." At least Emma could reassure her of that. "I'm not sure we're even friends anymore. The whole thing is just a mess."

Harriet sighed. "I was just thinking today that there might be someone else I hadn't considered before. Someone kind, and caring, and right here. I know you blame yourself for pointing out the long distance problem between Martin and me, but you didn't create it. It's not imaginary. The problem still exists."

"Who?" Emma couldn't help asking. "Who hadn't you

considered before?"

Harriet blushed. "George. I watched him take such good care of Betty at the party, and he's so nice. I think we might get along really well. It doesn't hurt that he's handsome, too. Would that be weird for you, Emma? I know the two of you have been friends for such a long time."

"George is a good guy," Emma managed to say. She hadn't expected this, and yes, it would be incredibly weird for so many reasons.

"What should I do? You know him better than I do." Harriet leaned forward.

Emma met her eager expression with what she hoped was a good poker face, pressing her lips together and desperately trying to think of what to say. Harriet expected her to giggle and plot with her on how they might get them together. What kind of monster had Emma created? She didn't want Harriet and George to fall in love. Jealousy raged up like a dragon awoken from a long sleep, creating a mix of guilt and frustration she desperately didn't want Harriet to see on her face.

The old Emma would have tactfully moved Harriet in another direction from pursuing George, or come up with reasons why he wasn't right for her, maybe even flat-out invented a girlfriend for him. But Emma had to leave that part of herself behind.

The fact was, Harriet probably was a better match for George. They were both kind and caring, and Harriet's bubbly personality made a good foil for George's more subdued one. But Emma should not and definitely would not volunteer to help.

"Harriet, I totally overstepped with Martin and with Elton. I think it's best if we don't discuss this."

"Oh." Harriet's face fell, and when Emma didn't say anything else, she picked up her purse. "I see what you mean. Goodnight, Emma." With a stiff set to her shoulders, she got up and left. Perhaps in her excitement over George she'd forgotten Emma's awful confession, or maybe she recognized Emma was the unwilling gatekeeper to getting closer to George, and by refusing to get involved, Emma was keeping her from him. And more than anything, Emma did want to keep Harriet from George.

She suddenly felt cold all over, and her clothes tight and scratchy. Fleeing to her room, she changed into pajamas and washed off her makeup. The circles under her eyes looked deeper than usual, the result of a sleepless night. Tonight would likely be no different.

George had made it more than clear he only wanted to be friends. But could Emma just hand him over to Harriet and wish them joy? No matter what she did or didn't do, it felt like it would be meddling. Self-improvement shouldn't be this confusing.

Turning her thoughts to caring for Granddad, she served up the dinner Harriet had left in the crockpot and asked him about his day. They played a quick game of Yahtzee, with Emma doing the scoring—entirely too much math in Emma's opinion. Then, with him off to bed, she called up Isabella to make sure she was all right. The contractions had stopped, thank goodness.

Emma was relieved for Isabella, but also for herself. She wasn't ready to face George yet. Telling Harriet had been hard enough, and now there were new problems making things even stickier. She needed to get things straight in her head and fix this mess she'd created, the mess he still didn't know about. She'd tell him everything, eventually. Right now, she didn't know if she could bear any more of his disappointment.

CHAPTER 15 ♥ THE MOST UNWILLING ACCOMPLICE OF ALL TIME

Harriet gave Emma a strained smile when she saw her the next morning, and Emma's heart sank. Given time to think about it, Harriet must have fully awakened to what Emma had done, and she probably regretted mentioning George at all.

They didn't chat as they normally did. Emma didn't want to force unwanted conversation on her even if she could think of what to say.

Deciding to give Harriet space, Emma gathered up her things, though her first appointment wasn't for another hour, kissed Granddad on the cheek, said goodbye, and left.

Having already eaten breakfast, she drove without a destination at first before remembering another person she needed to make amends with. She drove toward George's work, being careful to use the entrance away from the clinic. She didn't want George knowing she was here.

Weeks ago, she'd gotten Betty's address from George so she could send an official invitation for the murder mystery dinner party. The thank you cards that came with the kit were still sitting in a drawer by her bed. She'd sent three out, to Austin, Cara, and Nicole. The rest she kept putting off.

It took a little bit of wandering to find building B, and then, counting down the apartments, she found 342 and knocked, making sure to stand back and centered so that Betty, or Jane, or whoever answered could see her through the peephole.

What if it was Jane who answered? Emma owed her an apology too, but maybe mentioning the party would only dredge up something neither of them wanted to revisit. Did Betty want her shortcomings in acting brought up either? Or the fact that Emma had mockingly called her George's date? What was she even doing here with her lame practiced apology?

At the highest point in Emma's panic, the door opened, and Betty smiled brightly at her. Emma squared her shoulders. What would George want her to do?

Be a friend. Wasn't that what he'd been doing when he invited Betty in the first place?

"Hi, Betty. I'm sorry to just drop by like this. I had some time before work this morning and thought of you and wondered how you were doing. We didn't get to know each other very well at the party, and George thinks so highly of you." She was babbling, but luckily Betty took pity on her and ushered her inside and over to the tiny kitchen table, getting her a cold bottle of water from the fridge.

"I hope I'm not a bother," Emma said, glancing around before she sat. Betty had a good sense of organization for such a small space. She'd added floating bookshelves where she kept essentials like mixing bowls and pitchers. They were too ordinary to be mere decoration, but she'd arranged them to look decorative.

"It's not much. Your home is so beautiful."

Emma stopped staring at the walls. Betty must have assumed she was judging. "It's not really my home. It's Grandad's. For as grumpy as he is, he hates to live alone. I moved back after college. My sister had a newborn and a toddler, and it was too much for her to care for him all by herself. Anyway, I was just admiring your shelves. You've used this space well."

Betty glanced at the floor. "Thank you."

"And your mother lives here, right?"

"Yes, but she's not dressed yet. It would embarrass her to meet you without her teeth in and her hair done."

Emma bit her nail. "Yes, of course." She really should have

112

given Betty notice. What a rude way to start off trying to be friends. "I'm sorry I dropped in on you unexpectedly. Maybe we could exchange phone numbers so the next time I come you'll know ahead of time."

Betty's eyes widened slightly. "We could certainly do that." She slid out a drawer and pulled out a pen and a notepad.

Emma had just said 'next time.' Maybe that was a tad presumptuous. But if she was committing to changing old habits, that also meant following through on good intentions and not adding them to her pile of forgotten hobbies, like the knitting. Matchmaking was hopefully the last hobby she'd drop on that pile.

Betty slid the pad of paper across the table, and Emma wrote her name and number after adding Betty's to her contacts list.

"Jane's at work?" Emma asked. She took a small sip from the water bottle Betty had given her.

Betty glanced around nervously. "No, she's not." She sat in the chair next to Emma and leaned in. "I wasn't sure whether to call George and explain. I promised Jane I wouldn't. Oh, he'll be so disappointed in me, and if neither of you wants to talk to me again I wouldn't blame you at all. I'm sure they're scrambling at the clinic, and it's all my fault because I pressed Jane to get a job there. I promise I'll tell George when this all shakes out. Don't say anything first, will you?"

Emma shook her head. "Don't worry about that. I haven't talked to George much lately anyway. But I'm not sure I understand. What happened to Jane?"

"She's gone, though her things are still here. She said she was taking a couple of sick days and driving to Sacramento."

"To see Finn?"

Betty wrinkled her nose. "I called my sister and asked about him. She said he and Jane have been like Romeo and Juliet since high school, except not with the poison and daggers and all that. Madly in love, then they break up just to get together again."

"I thought they were friends." Even as she said it, Emma knew it wasn't true. Nobody had bought that, especially not George, who seemed to see everything.

"That's what she told us, but really he was the ex-boyfriend she left behind to move here. My sister thinks Jane hoped he would follow, and he did. She made it easy for him. Finn's dad lives not too far from our apartment, you see."

"Ahh." That was the craziest thing Emma had ever heard. She was itching to call Nicole and Cara and tell them about it, but she whacked that idea over the head. She was turning a new leaf and all that. She couldn't even tell George since she'd promised she wouldn't. "Is Jane coming back?"

Betty shrugged. "That's what I need to find out today." Her mother coughed from one of the bedrooms and called softly for Betty.

Emma slid out her chair and stood. "I'll let you go. Thank you so much for talking with me."

Betty nodded, looking embarrassed. "It was nice of you to come, even if it's just this once. I'm sure George appreciates your efforts." She rushed from the room to check on her mother and came back a minute later, looking surprised to see Emma still standing there.

Emma gripped the water bottle in her hand, feeling stupid but also stubbornly resolute in winning Betty over. Betty still thought Emma didn't like her. First impressions were hard to overcome. "I'm sorry for the things I said at the party. Truly. And actually, George doesn't know I'm here, and I don't want him to know. You won't tell him?"

Betty's face softened. "I won't tell him. Poor George is being kept in the dark about a lot of things right now, I guess."

"He'll be all right." Emma thought back to the firm way he'd insisted they go back to being friends. She was still mad at him for that, whether he was right about it or not. "I was thinking, would you like to have lunch tomorrow? I have an appointment nearby, and I could just as easily bring something to your apartment for all of us to eat, rather than sitting by myself in my car."

"If you're sure, I'd love that. What time?"

Emma pulled up her calendar and they planned the details. With a much lighter heart, she went off to work.

***

114

"She's still not here?" George glanced around Lois's desk, as if Jane might pop out from a hiding place behind the file cabinets or something. But that wasn't going to happen.

Lois pointed toward Dr. Perry's little office. "Ask him. She called again a few minutes ago and said she wasn't coming in after all and asked to talk to him. Please have her quit or fire her already. I can't take any more of this millennial wishy-washy nonsense."

It was nothing George wasn't aware of, but it wasn't his call to make, and he didn't have time to find out what Jane's hourly status was from Dr. Perry. "Never mind, I have patients waiting. You can put Alice Bettany in room six. I'll be in after my ten o'clock."

"You got it." Lois hollered for Alice, and he went in to see his next patient, an impatient man who just needed a medication refill and resented having to be seen every three months to get it.

It was days like this that made George dream of a tropical vacation somewhere, hiking through the jungle down a path to a private beach while a light rain mist fell on them. Them. Dang it. He'd placed Emma there with him. In his fantasy, she was ahead of him on the trail, glancing back with a mischievous smile. In vain, he tried to erase her from the scene.

George kneaded his forehead and forced his mind to other things. He got the man his refill, discovered Alice had shingles, got the poor woman a prescription, and disinfected the office, though there was little chance of anyone contracting chicken pox unless an infant happened to crawl in.

He was about to leave for his lunch break when Lois called him up front. "There's some girl and an old man here to see you. They brought you lunch."

Emma?

He walked out, only to see Harriet Smith and Mr. Woodhouse. Harriet held a deli meal in a plastic dome tray out toward him like a gift. "They just put in that specialty market across the street. Mr. Woodhouse mentioned your office was over here, and you usually had your lunch break at noon, so we

115

thought we'd run by and bring you something."

Mr. Woodhouse glanced around and scratched his ear. "Don't put this on me. It was all her idea. But we ought to get the milk home, don't you think?"

Harriet patted Mr. Woodhouse's arm. Her face was serene, if a little pink with embarrassment. "The milk will hold for a few minutes."

George smiled. "Thank you. That's so nice of you to think of me." And a little suspect. Harriet's expectant face stayed on him, as if she were reading his every reaction and analyzing it. That was not something a woman did for an impulsive gesture. Not to mention that Mr. Woodhouse had already outed himself as the most unwilling accomplice of all time. George highly doubted Mr. Woodhouse actually mentioned the location of George's office or his lunch hour. No, this had to be Emma's encouragement.

It was like a kick to the gut. She'd taken his advice about Elton not being a solid prospect for Harriet and decided maybe George was. Emma must have really talked him up to get Harriet this excited. The thought turned his stomach.

But, regardless of motives, it was nice of them to bring him lunch, and he made a few more minutes of small talk, noting the way Harriet's eyes lit up anytime he revealed anything about himself, even as inconsequential as his preference for rainy weather.

He hated eating in the office, so once they were gone, he headed to his own car and drove to a nearby park. Inside the plastic lid was a roasted chicken meal with a side of mashed potatoes and corn—comfort food at its best.

Unfortunately, every bite was a reminder of Emma's stubborn insistence on matchmaking. If ever there were a signal Emma only wanted to be friends, trying to set him up had to be it. How did everything go so wrong?

CHAPTER 16 ♥ A CRASH-COURSE IN PARENTING

When George squinted at his ringing phone, registering a call from John, and the time, three-thirty in the morning, he knew what it meant.

"John, is Isabella okay?"

"The baby's coming for real this time."

"I'll be there in five minutes."

"No need. We took the kids to Emma's on our way to the hospital. Just pray for us."

"I will."

John hung up, and George rolled out of bed before he could change his mind. He needed to make sure Emma and the kids were okay. If she wasn't getting any sleep, neither would he.

Besides, it was Saturday. His only set plan had been to sort through the resumes Dr. Perry had emailed him. They would be much more careful this time around with hiring Jane's replacement.

George still didn't fully understand why she'd left, and she didn't explain other than to say she was returning to Sacramento for good. Betty confirmed that she'd moved back for Finn. That seemed like the worst decision ever, but he truly hoped she'd be happy.

He drove over to the Woodhouse's and used his key to get

in, hoping he wouldn't scare Emma by not alerting her. She and Mr. Woodhouse had one spare bedroom, and he tiptoed in there, where Emma, Johnny, and Emmy, her little namesake, were curled up together on the queen bed. The image sunk deep into his heart, awakening things he'd promised himself he'd let go of.

He retreated to the den and stopped short. Emma had rearranged the furniture, and it took him a second to locate the blanket basket tucked behind the couch. Pulling the longest blanket over him, he made a makeshift bed.

John had not texted with any updates. Maybe he was afraid of waking him again. George would just have to text him.

I'm at Emma's. Send an update when you can.

He put his phone away and had almost drifted to unconsciousness when there was a long wail from down the hall.

George threw the blanket off himself and bolted to the guest bedroom, only to collide with Emma in the doorway. Their legs tangled, and he wrapped his arms around her as they hit the floor, and some sharp part of her hit him squarely in the chest, probably her chin.

She screamed and pushed off of him, not knowing who he was.

"Emma, it's me. It's George."

"Oh," she collapsed with relief right back down to his chest, and over the sound of their heavy breathing he listened to see if they'd awoken the whole house.

"Never scare me like that again," she whispered. Her heart was pounding, and he felt it slow a little, to about the pace of his heart, though his was starting to pick up the longer she stayed on top of him.

Her head cocked to the side like a little bird. "Nobody's crying."

She was right.

They both squinted in the dark in the direction of the bedroom and saw two little people staring at them from the bed where they were kneeling at the edge.

Emmy giggled. "Are you two gonna kiss?"

Johnny covered his eyes.

"Well, that's one way to stop him from crying." Emma crawled off of George and rubbed her chin. "That rattled my jaw pretty good. How's your head?"

He hadn't noticed the throbbing with his attention elsewhere, but when he felt the top of his head, there was a nice goose egg, painful to the touch, from where his head hit the hallway baseboard.

Emma reached up and felt his head, too. He froze, not wanting to even wince. The last time she'd tried to touch his hair he'd pulled away from her, and he had seen the hurt it caused. He couldn't give her any more mixed signals. It wasn't good for either of them. Being this close to her was its own special kind of torture, but it didn't change that they couldn't be together. His head knew it, even if his heart was having trouble accepting it.

"Back to bed, you two," George said as soon as Emma stepped away from him. He exaggeratingly lifted his knees and tiptoed into the bedroom with his arms out like some cartoon villain, stalking the kids until they giggled and slid off the bed, squealing and looking for places to hide.

"George, they're never going back to sleep now."

He lifted up a corner of the quilt covering the bed, pretending to look for them. "Probably not. What's the plan?"

Emma yawned. "Johnny wanted water." She squeezed her eyes shut and blinked. "That's where I was headed when you clobbered me."

George resisted the urge to pull her into a hug. She looked so tired. "I'll get him water, and I'll take them into the den and turn on a show. I saw you had a hot air balloon channel the other day. Did you know that? Nothing but scenes of hot air balloons floating by. They'll love it. You go back to bed and try to get some decent sleep. At seven, we'll switch."

She was tired enough that she didn't fight him on it.

***

Emma sat straight up in bed and covered her ear. What had just

119

happened? A bad dream?

But then Johnny's quiet giggling alerted her to his presence. He was crouching by the side of her bed, and she reached out a hand and felt his little head.

"Johnny, did you stick your finger in my ear? Where's George?"

"Aseep."

Of course he was. Emma threw back her covers and took Johnny's little hand as they walked down the hall and into the den. Both Emmy and George were asleep, while the TV still showed images of hot air balloons flying over a meadow.

"How long have you been awake?" Emma whispered to Johnny. "Are you hungry for breakfast?"

"I ate." Johnny tugged on her arm and led her into the kitchen. He proudly pointed to the open bread box and the stool he'd pushed over there to get up on the counter. He'd helped himself to the middles of several pieces of bread, leaving the crusts and the open bread bag half dumped out.

"What else have you been up to?" Emma asked. She glanced at the microwave clock. Six thirty. Depending on whether Johnny ever fell back to sleep at all, that was a lot of time for mischief.

"I was wet." He pointed to his pajama pants. They were on backward, and he was sporting a bit of a plumber's crack.

"Where's your diaper?" Emma's eyes widened.

Johnny shrugged. "I take it off." He snapped the waistband of his pajama pants and grinned, clearly pleased he'd been able to put the pajamas back on himself after ditching the diaper.

Emma picked him up, relieved that his pajama pants were still dry, and carried him back to the den. She searched the large duffle bag John had brought in with the kids until she found the diapers. Mid-diaper change, she glanced at the couch and realized George was no longer there.

"George?" she called as loudly as she dared.

He popped his head out of the half bathroom off the den. "I hate to tell you this, but there's a diaper in the toilet, and if I'm not mistaken, that little monster had something to do with it."

"Moster?" Johnny asked.

"Just you, buddy." Emma helped him to his feet.

He reached down and patted the crinkly material of his new diaper.

"From now on, only I take off your diapers. And no toilets. You stay away from those."

"Banned?" Johnny asked.

"Yes, you're banned."

"How does he know that word?" George asked.

"It's a long story. Is the toilet okay?"

"He didn't flush it. If that were the case, we'd probably be calling a plumber. But those little diaper beads escaped everywhere. You wanna bring me some plastic gloves and a trash bag?"

"I'm on it." She pulled three matchbox cars out of the duffle bag and handed them to Johnny. "Stay right here, buddy. Promise?"

He nodded, already running the cars along the length of the couch.

She ran and got the gloves and trash bag from the cabinets under the kitchen sink, and grabbed a container of disinfectant wipes as well. Before she could decide whether he might need some type of strainer to capture all the errant beads, there was an angry moan that sounded like Emmy being woken up. Emma ran back in with the supplies, and sure enough, in the thirty seconds she'd been gone, Johnny had decided to use his sister as a race track.

George came out of the bathroom holding an armful of towels. "Sorry, I should have been watching him. We should wash these. He pulled all the towels off the racks and I think they got sprinkled with toilet water."

Emma hung her head. "Isabella must be a ninja or something. How does she do it?" Leaving the gloves, trash bag, and disinfectant wipes on the bathroom counter, Emma relieved George of his towel burden and headed to the laundry room. Emmy followed, asking for breakfast.

Would the whole day be like this? Emma yawned and started a load of towels, washed her hands, and got Emmy breakfast. In a moment of panic, she realized she didn't know what Johnny was up to and ran back to find him and George playing cars on the floor.

George laughed at her panicked face, knowing exactly what she'd been thinking.

Despite the craziness of the morning, working as a team like this had succeeded in eliminating the awkwardness between them. Emma hoped it wasn't a temporary truce. There was no one else in the world she'd rather embark with on a crash-course in parenting.

She still wasn't sure what to do about Harriet, but for the weekend at least, she could set that aside. A lot depended on whether George had any interest in Harriet. He'd been awfully concerned with whether or not Emma was treating her well, and he hadn't liked Harriet flirting with Elton at the party. Was that interest?

What if it was? Emma's chest tightened at the thought. The mature thing would be to accept George's request for friendship and let the thought of anything else go. Emma didn't feel like being mature.

Emma had never liked any of George's girlfriends, but she'd always told herself it was because they weren't right for him. Had it always been jealousy, even before she was aware of her feelings for him?

If it wasn't Harriet, someday it would be someone else. Emma wasn't blind to the way women looked at George. What would happen when some lucky woman snatched him up, and he didn't have time for the two of them anymore? They'd still see each other since Isabella was married to his brother, but maybe this weekend was the last of its kind.

These morbid thoughts were not helping. She was already sleep deprived and needed to be on her game. Her focus should be on the kids. Putting away the milk and rinsing the dishes, she quizzed Emmy on what she might like to do today. The little girl stopped mid-sentence in her answer as George came running into the kitchen with Johnny in one arm and his phone in the other.

"Girls, look!"

"Baby," Johnny said proudly, pointing to George's phone.

"Oh." Emma dropped the dishrag she'd been holding, and George bent down so the four of them could all see together.

Announcing George Edison Knightley. Born at 5:45 a.m. 4 pounds, 12 ounces. We'll be in the NICU for a while but all are well.

George's namesake was tiny, and red, and absolutely perfect. Emma felt like her heart grew ten times over just looking at him. Her eyes turned to George, and she softly pressed a kiss to his cheek, leaving her lips there for a moment. Not wanting to ruin the moment with reading into any reaction he might or might not have, she left their little celebratory circle and went to find her phone so she could call Isabella.

CHAPTER 17 ♥ LIKE A SLEEPOVER

George pulled his arm out from under Johnny's pillow, slowly, slowly, slowly. Johnny stirred in his sleep, but his eyes stayed shut. In the doorway, Emma stood stock still, watching. It had been a long day, and if all went well, when George lifted his weight from the bed they'd be free, maybe until morning.

He waited a minute and then slid back until he was off the bed, hovering at the same height in case Johnny opened his eyes and caught him trying to leave.

After another twenty seconds he tiptoed out to Emma, and they practically ran from the room.

"Nice ninja skills, George."

"Thanks." He followed her to the kitchen where she slid out a package of Oreos from a hiding spot in an upper cupboard. He'd discovered she had lots of those all over the house.

"Hitting the hard stuff, huh?"

She opened the fridge and got out the milk. "After a day like today, I think three perfect Oreos dipped in milk is exactly what I need."

He helped himself to a few and took a bite. "You did amazing today. I was impressed."

She started to smile at his words, but then let out a long sigh. "Exceeded your expectations, did I?" The words sounded a little bitter.

George took the cup of milk she offered him and didn't dare

say anything else. This sounded like the beginnings of an argument where he'd end up sleeping on the couch. Oh, the irony.

Emma waved a cookie at him. "I'm sorry. You were trying to be nice, and I did that thing girls do." She slid the two halves of her cookie apart and dipped the half missing the cream in her milk. "Where we take a compliment as an opportunity to be insecure about ourselves."

"No, you're right. I lecture too much." His kids, if he ever had any, would hate it.

"In my case, I need it." Emma rubbed her forehead and then checked her fingers. "Did I just rub Oreo crumbs on myself?"

George took a step toward her to check. He didn't see anything, but he rubbed his thumbs across to her temples anyway. Tonight felt like the last hurrah before he backed off for good and let Emma be the confident, amazing person she was, without his interference. She needed his friendship, not the brooding, jealous guy he'd been lately.

Her eyes met his and softened. "Thank you for fishing diaper beads out of a toilet, and climbing up on a ladder to rescue Johnny's teddy bear from the roof. Oh, and letting Emmy put makeup on you with her Minnie Mouse fashion kit."

George examined his fingernails. "Thank you for not taking any pictures of that and lending me the nail polish remover. I'm not a fan of glitter on my nails."

"Poor Emmy was a little scared by Granddad's vehement no. You made her day when you said she could give you a makeover instead." Emma moved away with the Oreo package and put it back in its hiding spot. "We should get sleep while we can."

"Yeah, you're right." Though he would have been happier to stay up with her, he put the milk carton away and swept up any incriminating cookie crumbs with his hand.

They stared at each other, neither making a move to leave, and Emma smiled. "Maybe one episode of *Cooking with Strangers*?"

George bit back a grin. "I'll meet you in the den in a minute. I'm gonna change into flannel pants and brush my teeth first."

***

George made it sound like a sleepover. The butterflies in Emma's stomach kicked up at the thought. No. She couldn't think that way. He was sleeping in the den, and he tended to doze off while watching TV. It made sense for him to get ready for bed. That was all.

Emma hurried down the hall to her room and changed into her softest pajamas before brushing her teeth and brushing out her hair. A strange part of her felt disloyal to Harriet, though it didn't make any sense. She really had created some conflicts of interest with her matchmaking, hadn't she? It wasn't Emma's job to find Harriet love, and it wasn't her duty to keep George at arms-length, though she probably should. Every time they got close to each other, everything got confusing and ended up threatening their friendship.

It would help if she knew how George felt, but if he did have feelings for Harriet, Emma doubted he'd tell her. She'd have to watch for clues.

Dragging her favorite blanket off her bed, she jogged to the den and plopped down on one end of the couch.

"You rearranged the furniture in here." He looked down at the blanket piled between them and then over to the loveseat now in the corner, the one they used to cuddle on.

"You don't like it?" She could not admit the real reason she'd done it, though there was little chance she'd ever be sandwiched between George and Elton again.

"It's great. It took me by surprise, is all." He kicked out his footrest and leaned the seat back, pulling his own blanket over himself.

She reluctantly did the same on her side, keeping the three-foot distance between them. She hated every inch of it, but this was what he'd asked for.

He had the remote and pointed it at the TV, but he stopped before hitting play and set it on his lap. "Harriet brought me lunch the other day."

Emma gripped her blanket. "She did?"

"I'm not sure how she got my number, but she texted me

126

later to see if I liked it."

Emma sat up straighter at that part. How did Harriet get his number? Had she gotten into Emma's phone? She wouldn't do that, would she?

"Emma."

She looked over at George, not sure what he wanted from her. Acceptance? Acknowledgment? "Did you text her back?" she asked.

George hit play on the TV. "Just to thank her." His face was so unreadable.

Waves of jealousy crashed into each other. Emma hadn't expected Harriet to be so assertive. The girl was serious about her interest in George, and apparently, secretive.

She considered times where Harriet might have had access to her phone before it occurred to her George's cell number was listed on the fridge with the other emergency numbers for Granddad. That was a relief. Harriet must have seen his number there. Much less stalkery.

If Harriet was pursuing him in earnest, he needed to know what happened to Elton. He had to be wondering.

Emma reached over and stole the remote from George's lap, pausing the show in the middle of their dramatic delay of reading the results.

She stared at George for several seconds, and he stuck his tongue out at her.

"What is it, Emma? Planning to confess?"

Hesitating, she finally scooted over and tucked herself under his blanket, sharing his footrest. Forget physical boundaries. They could return to those later. "You were so right about Elton," she whispered.

"What happened?" George asked. He adjusted so the blanket fully covered both of them.

"He came over one night and asked me out. He had no interest in Harriet."

"But he had interest in you." George didn't sound surprised.

"Yeah. I told him that wasn't going to happen."

"Good," George said gruffly. He adjusted until he was on his side, his body facing hers. Waves of heat came off him, and

127

Emma felt goosebumps erupt all over her. She was in love with him. She knew it now. But the fear of being rejected ate her up inside, making her want to hide those feelings from him where he'd never see them. He didn't think she was right for him.

"Elton was so sure I was interested in him. I don't think he'll come over anymore and try to watch TV with us." Emma shrugged, the embarrassment of it all coming back.

"Emma, promise me something." George's face was the perfect amount of stubbly.

She nodded, her fingers itching to reach out and stroke his jaw.

"Promise me you won't interfere in my love life anymore."

That was like a cold splash of water in the face. Emma turned away from him, pulling her half of the blanket tight. "I won't. I promise." They'd crashed and burned, and he probably wanted to make sure he and Emma never came close to moving beyond friendship again. With all his mentions of Harriet, maybe he was preparing her for what would happen next. Now that she thought about it, all of George's previous girlfriends had been the assertive types. Those two really were made for each other.

Well, she wouldn't humiliate herself by moving back to her side of the couch, despite his warning. He'd just have to deal with the close proximity for now.

She turned the show back on, where the camera panned from couple to nail-biting couple. Donny and Denise were eliminated. Of course, they were. Tears pricked her eyes, and in panic, she held as still as possible. She couldn't cry. George would think she was crying over Donny and Denise. She suddenly hated this stupid show. Her head hurt, and the strain of the day made her limbs ache. Grabbing a couch pillow, she tucked it under her head and rested her eyes for a minute.

***

George blinked in the hazy morning light flickering through the blinds. It took him a moment to remember where he was and why. He was so warm. The heat was emanating from under his arm, where to his surprise and slight alarm, Emma lay. They'd both fallen asleep. He remembered shutting off the TV, but that was about it.

"Psst. Hey."

George turned to see John standing in the doorway to the den, looking both amused and shocked. How long had he been standing there? "George, what the heck, dude. That's my sister-in-law."

George pulled away from Emma, not that it made the situation look any better. "We fell asleep watching TV."

"Well, obviously. But, you two look a little cozy there. Did you two have a makeout sesh last night? Because the way you looked over at her before you realized I was here..." He slowly shook his head. "Dang, that means I owe Isabella a foot rub. I didn't think you had it in you, but she said it was inevitable."

Emma yawned and rubbed her eyes. "John, we did not have a makeout sesh. And that's not the way you greet the two people who've been keeping your kids alive. How's the baby?"

John stuck his hands in his pockets. "He's amazing. But he has to maintain weight and body temperature goals and get off oxygen before they'll let us take him home. Isabella wanted me to check in with you guys and play with the kids for a little bit. Are they still asleep?"

Emma and George exchanged glances. They had no idea.

John waved a dismissive hand at them. "Stay there and snuggle. I'll go find my kids."

Emma sat up and stretched, and George did the same.

"Are you done with the blanket?" he asked.

She nodded and pushed it off of her legs. The awkwardness was back, and it wasn't because of John's teasing. She looked sad. Maybe he'd hurt her feelings over the matchmaking thing, disappointed that he wasn't interested in Harriet.

George let out a sigh, reminding himself, again, that no matter how good of friends they were, or how much he wanted more, it didn't change things. He couldn't think of anything worse than pining after someone who hoped to set him up with her friends.

There was little time to dwell on it. The kids were so excited to see John that they ran all over the house screaming, which was not Mr. Woodhouse's favorite way to be woken up. John had them so riled up at breakfast with airplane rides and bear attacks that Johnny dropped his syrupy plate on the floor and Emmy spilled her milk across the table

John was not Mr. Woodhouse's favorite person on a good day. Not only had he up and married Isabella, causing her to leave home, but he had a way of making everything around him louder and more intense. It made him a great older brother and a fun dad, but George sighed in relief when John left to return to the hospital. Things could go back to being a little more structured.

George took the kids outside, and Emma took on the task of soothing Granddad and gathering Emmy and Johnny's toys and clothes.

Mom was flying in that afternoon and would take the kids to John and Isabella's house. Their babysitting gig was almost up. George was relieved, but a little sad, too. After this, how often would he and Emma really see each other? Until he could get his head on straight, he didn't think it would be wise to keep coming over.

CHAPTER 18 ♥ HAND IN THE COOKIE JAR

Emma jogged up to Betty's door with her bags of thrift store clothes, excited with what she'd found.

What she did for a living had eventually come up in their conversations, despite Emma's reluctance to mention it. The topic of makeovers and fashion often made people feel uncomfortable, or worse, obligated to ask if they needed one. Emma was not in the business of pushing her fashion advice where it wasn't wanted. Especially now that she was trying to withhold her advice on anything.

Betty, however, thought it was exciting and immediately dragged Emma in to see her tiny closet where she'd organized her clothing by color—from drab on the left to garish on the right. She was on a fixed income with limited space, but she wanted help. Emma asked her to think about it for a few days, but she didn't forget or change her mind.

So, they struck a deal. Betty paid Emma in cooking lessons and baked goods, and Emma began replacing Betty's worn out clothing items a few at a time, stopping at thrift stores or consignment shops here and there when she had free time. Free time had become her nemesis. It was when her thoughts shifted to George. Oh, how she missed him.

They still texted, but he didn't offer to come over, and she didn't dare ask. They visited John and Isabella at the hospital at opposite times. She watched TV alone. She'd lost him, and it haunted her. It was a pit-in-the-stomach, gnawing regret that nipped at her heels like a badly behaved puppy. So, she stayed busy.

Today, she'd found a sidewalk sale where you could fill a whole bag for five dollars. She'd bought two full bags, washed everything, thrown out anything that still smelled or wrinkled into nothingness, and called Betty with the good news. The woman rarely was not free, poor soul, and they agreed to have lunch together and look through everything.

Betty answered right away when Emma knocked, clapping in excitement at the sight of Emma's finds.

It was not professional at all, but they dumped both bags out right there on Betty's couch and exclaimed over their finds without any particular rhyme or reason. Emma sighed, realizing it was because they were friends.

She'd thought Harriet was her friend, but that had been a relationship based too much on a balance of power, and the moment Emma stepped back from it, the bottom dropped out. They were still cordial, and Harriet and Granddad still got along famously, but it wasn't like before, and as awkward as that made things, it was probably for the best.

"Look at this one!" Betty held up a blouse and let the silky material flutter in her hands. "Should I try it on? I should go show Mother."

"Go for it."

The timer for the homemade pizza went off, and Emma turned on the oven light and peeked in. The cheese wasn't quite melty enough. She'd check it in a few minutes.

An extra bag of pizza dough was in the fridge to take home. Her payment from Betty for today. Hopefully, Granddad would like making pizza, too.

"Emma, would you get the door?" Betty called out.

Emma hadn't even heard a knock, but she went and checked the peephole. It was George. She touched her throat and turned in a circle, trying to think what to do.

***

132

George was about to walk off when the door cracked open, and Emma, of all people, poked her head out, looking like she'd been caught with her hand in the cookie jar.

"What are you doing here?" he asked. It was like his imagination had conjured her up from nowhere. He'd been thinking about her, and poof, there she was, beautiful and vibrant and raising her eyebrow at him, like he was the intruder.

"I'm having lunch with Betty." She opened the door wider so he could come in, though it was clear she was reluctant to do so.

When he saw the piles of clothes on the couch, everything started to come together. "You're giving her a makeover?" he whispered. "She's on a fixed income, and please tell me she did not become one of your projects."

He expected Emma to look guilty and irritated at being caught. But her face turned bright red, and she stepped right up to him, in all her five-foot-nothing frame. "You stop that right now." She was trembling with anger, and she swallowed and glanced toward Betty's bedroom. "She's not a project to me. Not even a little bit. You think you know everything about me, but all you see lately are the mistakes I've made. I get it. I've made a lot of them. Stop judging me for being here. She's my friend, too."

Betty stepped out from the hallway and raised her hand. "Let me stop you right there since I can hear you. I like you both, but you have this strange habit of dragging me into your arguments, my dears."

"Sorry, Betty," Emma said meekly.

George ran a hand through his hair. "I'm sorry, too. I actually came to check on your mother. Is that okay?"

Betty nodded. "Of course. And please stay for lunch."

George, feeling like an idiot, picked up his medical bag and escaped to the bedroom. From the sound of it, Emma and Betty went back to sorting clothes, discussing the potential of each item and laughing together as if he'd never come.

Mrs. Bates had been asleep, but she opened her eyes and turned to look at George when he touched her shoulder. He talked softly to her while he checked her over. Betty took such good care of her that he didn't have to worry about bedsores or

133

hygiene, though she was spending more and more of her time sleeping these days.

Emma laughed from the other room, and Mrs. Bates smiled. "Did you meet Emma?" she asked. "Such a nice girl. Burns everything she cooks, but she's found some pretty things for my Betty to wear."

"Emma's here a lot?"

"More lately. It's nice to hear Betty laugh again." She sat up and took a sip of water with George's assistance and then sighed and her eyes drifted shut.

He sat, trying to think, trying to figure Emma out. He did judge her too easily, but it was hard not to when he was still being bombarded with texts from Harriet with invitations to get together. He'd politely turned her down each time, but the woman was persistent, and he didn't have it in him to tell her off once and for all. If she texted hello, he texted back. But Emma was another story. He wanted to know why she hadn't put a stop to it like he'd asked.

From the other room, he could hear their conversation.

"I love this shirt," Emma said. "It was missing a button but I found a perfect match in my button bag."

Betty made a noise of agreement. "Buttons are so fun to collect. They're practical and they don't take up space, but I just like looking at them and running them through my hands. Is that silly?"

"Not silly at all. My mother had a button collection, and Granny found me playing with it when I was ten. I thought I was in trouble, but she gave me the whole bag. I've been collecting buttons ever since."

George had never heard that story. Emma rarely ever talked about the loss of her parents. It also occurred to him if she was replacing buttons on shirts, these items she'd found were not from her normal boutique, high-end places. And how did Mrs. Bates know Emma burned everything?

"The pizza!" Emma squeaked.

George came out of the bedroom, just in time to see Emma fanning the pizza before pulling it out of the oven.

"Oh, you're just a little bit crispy," she whispered to it. "Just

134

a little brown."

He and Betty exchanged glances and Emma caught them. "I checked it when the timer went off, but it wasn't ready yet."

"It looks delicious," Betty assured her.

The three sat at the table to eat, and for a few minutes, there was no need to talk as they sliced it up and divided the pieces.

Betty spoke first. "I'll just say in Emma's defense, I was the one who asked if she'd give me a closet consult. I wore her down with my begging, I'm afraid. It's not like I had anything to pay her with."

Emma smiled at her fondly. "I beg to differ. Thanks to your baking lessons, I can make granddad's favorite cookies."

George rested his chin on his hand. It was a good performance, but he still wasn't convinced this wasn't a pet project for her, benevolent as it may be.

"Harriet asked me out to dinner," he said, turning his water glass to catch the light from the tiny kitchen window.

Betty rolled her eyes and glanced at Emma, who looked … discouraged. So the two of them had discussed this.

"Why did you try to set her up with me, Emma? And why haven't you stopped?"

"I had nothing to do with it." She put down her pizza slice. "After the Elton disappointment, she launched straight into her admiration of you. I was shocked and didn't know what to say. I'd promised myself I wouldn't meddle anymore. So, I didn't tell her not to, but I swear to you I didn't encourage her. I told her I had to stay out of it."

"But you gave her my number and told her where I work and when I take my lunch break."

"No, I did not." Emma glanced at Betty. "In fact, I think I offended her when I bowed out of helping her. Harriet and I barely talk anymore. Sometimes I hide out here in the mornings before my appointments start."

"So, you didn't…" George rubbed his mouth. He did jump to conclusions and wrongly judge, didn't he? So convinced of Emma's guilt, he'd assumed the worst about all her motives. He felt like a jerk.

"Then you have no interest in Harriet?" Betty asked. She

135

gave Emma a smug smile, almost an I-told-you-so.

"Of course not."

"Because you're in love with someone else?"

His eyes darted to Emma, and then he looked away. He didn't deserve her. "Betty, I think you're enjoying this too much."

She laughed. "More than you know. It's okay though, because Emma's in love with you, too." She got up from her chair. "I'm just gonna go check on Mother."

CHAPTER 19 ♥ I HAPPEN TO LIKE IDIOTS

"And I thought you were the matchmaker." George shook his head. Emma loved the splash of red overtaking his face and the twinkle in his eyes that told her Betty, that little imp, had been right about both of them.

Emma's heart was going to beat right out of her chest as they stared at one another.

"So," she said.

"So," George said. "I uh, have to return to work. Could I come over later?"

Emma's throat was so dry, all she could do was nod.

He stood up and hesitated, before walking out the door, giving her one last backward glance that melted her insides into a puddle of anticipation.

"Betty," she squeaked out.

Betty came out of the bedroom, her hands clasped together. "Sorry, Emma. But the two of you were taking way too long to muddle through this thing. I couldn't help giving it a little push. Are you mad?"

Emma shook her head. "I'm not mad. But what do I say to Harriet?"

Betty shook her head. "I have no advice for that bit. I've meddled enough as it is, and we both know the trouble it causes."

"That I do." Emma's insides were still quivering, thinking

about George, but there were clothes to be sorted on Betty's couch and two appointments for later that afternoon.

However, it was a lot easier to plow through tasks with good thoughts dancing in the back of her head, rather than the gloom that had plagued her recently. Maybe she and George weren't doomed after all.

She helped Betty decide on the rest of the items and happily get rid of a few more things she'd never have to wear again. Then Emma left with her discard pile of clothes to donate on her way to her next appointment.

Normally, she dreaded working with this particular client. Kayleen Carothers was demanding and condescending, and this third appointment was Emma's last attempt to please her and get paid the second half of her fee. Otherwise, she'd eat the loss and cut ties with the woman forever.

"What are you smiling at?" Kayleen asked as she click-clacked up to Emma in her three-inch heels.

It was an accusation, not a greeting, and Emma quickly removed any joy from her face. It wasn't hard with the woman glaring at her.

The department store where Kayleen had insisted on meeting was not one where Emma had a strong relationship with the staff. At places like this, there was too much turnover for anyone to care who she was. She'd heard rumors that it would be closing soon, another victim of online shopping and the declining neighborhood. Already, the selections were sparser than the last time she'd come in.

But she took it all in stride and led the way over to the women's dress wear. "Are we still looking for a matching two-button jacket and pencil skirt?"

"Yes. And shoes to match. I also need a dress in dusty rose or sage for a wedding in two weeks. They sent their invitations out very late."

"No problem." It was a big problem, but what could she do? Kayleen had a huge prejudice against boutique stores and online shopping, so they'd see what this store had and go from there.

She wasted no time flipping through the racks and held up item after item, most of which were immediately rejected by

Kayleen.

While Kayleen was in the dressing room, Emma checked her phone. She'd heard the little buzz of an incoming text, and to her delight, it was George.

I'm an idiot.

I happen to like idiots. She quickly texted back.

Well, that's a relief.

Kayleen came out and Emma quickly hid her phone and her smile, but not before Kayleen saw. She frowned. "I was afraid you were too young for this job. Stay off social media and pay attention. Well, what do you think?" She turned in a circle in the jacket and skirt, and Emma scrunched her nose. It was passable business attire. Nothing special. It would need major alterations and made her look boxy.

"It's okay. I don't love it on you."

Kayleen sighed. "I was afraid you'd say that."

Emma tapped her side. "Can I ask why you hired me? You never take my advice on what would look good, and you don't want to go to any of the stores I suggest."

Kayleen smiled. "That right there is why I hired you. I don't need someone to cower before me and tell me everything looks great on me. I need brutal honesty."

"Well, to be honest, I don't think we'll find anything here. The one good jacket and skirt in the store is back on the rack. You said it looked like a zebra and a rhino had a baby and someone skinned it and turned it into a dress suit."

"I did say that, didn't I? Well, go fetch it, and I'll try it on."

Emma practically skipped back to the section they'd found it in and pulled the offending suit off the rack. Kayleen took it from her, holding it away from her body like it might bite her or something, but she went into the dressing room to try it on. Almost ten minutes went by, and when she came out, Emma knew that look on her face was as close to eating crow as the woman was going to get. While still being conservative, it stood out just enough to get her noticed, and it fit like it had been made for her body.

They bought the skirt and suit *and* found a dress for the wedding. By sheer luck, Emma was convinced. Kayleen paid her

139

in cash before they left the store.

By the time Emma returned home for the day, she was practically walking on air. Well, until she walked into the kitchen to face Harriet. It was time for them to have a talk. No more of this avoiding each other nonsense.

Granddad was working on a new puzzle. Harriet had set up a card table this time, and he had his headphones on, slightly swaying to the music. Occasionally he liked to listen to the old crooners.

There would never be a better opportunity. They could throw pots and pans around, and at the volume he had that music he'd never hear.

Taking Betty's lead, Emma decided to just be out with it. "Harriet, let's talk about George."

Harriet set down the mixing bowl she'd been drying and hunched her shoulders. "It's not working. I'm annoying him, aren't I?"

Emma pressed her hands into the counter. "I truly am sorry for everything I've said and done. I've been a terrible friend to you and an even worse boss. And with that said, not talking about any of this isn't helping us either. So, whatever I suggest, you can toss to the wind if you want."

Harriet gave her a small smile. "I've missed you, Emma. You never answered me when I asked if pursuing George would make things weird, and I accepted your deflection as permission. I'm a terrible friend and employee. So I guess we're even."

For some odd reason, Emma's eyes filled with tears. "I'm in love with him."

Harriet put her hands to her cheeks. "Oh, it's worse than I thought. Why didn't you tell me to back my turnip truck around and try some other field? I am so sorry."

"Don't be sorry. I think I was still in denial about it until you set your sights on him. In a way, you woke me up to it."

"Well, at least it was good for something. I've made a fool of myself. Martin's dating someone else, and I just desperately didn't want to be alone when he wasn't."

That only made Emma feel worse. She was the cause of Harriet's unhappiness. She hadn't wanted to see it, but Harriet had not been the same person since breaking up with Martin. Her cheery, carefree nature only came out in spurts now, like the sun trying to break through cloud cover.

"How do you know Martin's dating someone else?"

"He texted me and said he wished me the best, no hard feelings, and he'd started dating someone, and I shouldn't feel bad for wanting to move on. He was very sweet about it."

"He is a sweet guy, isn't he?"

Harriet nodded sadly. "I've never met anyone as genuine or as kind."

"Can you show me how to skip this song?" Granddad hollered from the other room, unaware of how loud he was with his headphones on.

Harriet rolled her eyes. "I'll be right back."

The second she left the room, Emma snatched up Harriet's phone from the counter, her heart galloping at the thought of what she was about to do.

The trusting girl didn't even have a password on her phone. How had Emma ever thought the reverse, that Harriet would break into her phone to steal a number? The irony of the moment was not lost on her.

Checking Harriet's contacts, she found Martin's number and typed it into her own messaging app. Then she quickly put the phone back in the same position on the counter.

CHAPTER 20 ♥ THE RIGHT MOMENT

George was a little later than usual, and he saw the relief in Emma's eyes when she let him in. But he hadn't wanted to show up smelling like work in the same clothes he'd worn all day. He'd ended up showering and shaving as well. When Emma turned around to lead him into the kitchen, he ran his hand across his baby soft jaw, hoping it wasn't patently obvious he was trying too hard.

Emma had mentioned once that she liked his cologne so he'd patted a little of that on, too. It wasn't something he thought about wearing all that much, but tonight seemed like a good night for it.

"Did you want something to eat?" she asked, opening and closing cupboards and then turning to open the fridge. She closed the fridge door seconds later and turned to look at him. Was she as nervous as he was?

"Don't worry about me," he assured her. "I'm not hungry."

This should be so easy now that they knew how they felt about one another, but if anything, he was more at a loss as to how to proceed. He'd been extremely rude and accusatory to her today, and he felt like he still owed her an apology. It just seemed like a lame way to start a conversation.

"How did you and Betty get to be such good friends?" he finally asked.

Emma leaned against the counter by the fridge and smiled.

"Hiding from Harriet. I'd wanted to apologize to Betty anyway for the way I acted at the party, but more than that, I wanted her to like me. She thought I was there because you asked me to. So, I kept coming, to prove to her I truly wanted to be her friend. And now we are friends."

"I know. I'm a huge jerk. You can say it."

Her eyes crinkled. "You're a huge jerk, George. Join the club."

He really wanted to kiss her. So much. But the moment wasn't quite right, and after waiting years he should probably not just accost her by the fridge.

"Oh, speaking of being a jerk, I need to run something by you." She pulled out her phone and came over to show him. "This is Martin's number."

"Why do you have that?" he asked as evenly as possible. He would not assume anything anymore ever, but the gleam in Emma's eyes was scaring him.

"I swear I'm retiring from matchmaking. But, he told Harriet he was dating someone, and I think he only said that to protect his feelings and help her move on. She can't ask him if it's true, but I can."

"Emma."

"Hear me out. If he is dating someone, I wish him luck, Harriet moves on, and she never knows I contacted him. But if not…"

"You don't need my permission, you know."

"This isn't permission. This is me being open and honest with you." She turned her dark blue eyes on him, looking solemn. "I'm sorry I hid what I was doing with Harriet and Elton."

He wrapped an arm around her, and she leaned her head in and rested it against his chest.

"I love you, Emma." The words came out in a whisper, but it felt good to get them out. "Betty beat me to it, but I thought I should actually say it to you."

She lifted her head to look at him. "I love you, too." Reaching up, she ran the back of her hand over his jawline and smiled. "You shaved. Any particular reason?"

143

"Because I wanted to."

"Pshaw. No man ever wants to shave. Was there another reason perhaps?"

He picked up a strand of her blonde hair from her shoulder and ran it through his fingers. "Are we talking cryptically again? What are you trying to say, Emma?"

Her lips pouted slightly. "Fine. I'll spell it out for you. I want you to kiss me, but I don't want to be the one to initiate it. Is that clear enough?"

He laughed. "I was waiting for the right moment."

She pulled away and went back to leaning against her counter by the fridge. "Whatever. Stall all you want. I'm a vault. When we're eighty and that right moment comes, just know I'll be ready for you."

She was such a tease. He shook his head. "Keep waiting, lady. I'll tell you a secret about men. They hate to be told what to do."

***

And yet he was coming toward her and his eyes were telling a different story. They said brace yourself for impact. Feeling hot and cold all over, Emma gripped the counter behind her just before his arms came around her waist, and his lips pressed down on hers—not hard, but not soft either. His kiss was persuasive, and frustrated, and laced with the strong emotions of someone who had been holding back for a very long time.

She met his kisses with a strong answer and strong emotions to match. Reaching up on her tiptoes, she let him hold her in place as she leaned into him, sighing between kisses and then coming in for more. She ran her fingers along the back of his neck where his hair was just starting to curl under. She'd finally gotten her opportunity to run her fingers through it.

He pulled away, and she groaned, resting her forehead against his jaw. "I kind of miss the scruff, to be honest."

"Don't worry, Emma. I'll be nice and scruffy tomorrow, and I'm really hoping this isn't the only time we do this."

"Not unless an asteroid comes down right now and takes us

144

out."

"Just in case then." He tilted his head and gave her another satisfyingly long and thorough kiss until she thought she might pass out with the sensations of it.

George pushed off from the counter behind them and let out a long breath. "Okay, distractions. Why don't you, um, contact Martin now and see what he says."

"Right now?"

"I could kiss you all night, Emma. I don't think you need to worry about me waiting for the right moment. Every moment until the end of time sounds pretty good right now."

Emma couldn't help blushing. "I never pegged you for a romantic, George."

"Is it a bad thing?"

"Um, not at all." She wrapped her arms around him and kissed along his jawline, loving the way his muscles tensed in reaction to her touch. He leaned down and captured her lips, and she was lost in him for several minutes before reluctantly pushing away. "Okay, texting Martin."

"Yes. Control freak George here wants to see what you're going to say."

She laughed, knowing it was true and loving that they could accept each other now, flaws and all.

She read it out loud as she typed. "Martin, sorry to bother you. This is a concerned friend of Harriet's. Whatever you respond with will not be seen by her. Are you really dating someone else?" She glanced at George. "Too much? Not enough? I don't want to spell out why I want to know unless he responds."

He nodded. "I think that works."

She shook out her arms and hit send. "No going back now."

They stared at her phone for several seconds as if Martin would instantly answer. No such luck. She put her phone away and dragged George to the den. "Help me rearrange the furniture again, will you? I hate having the couch squished against the wall."

"Why'd you change it all around in the first place?"

"Because I was afraid of what I felt when we cuddled

145

together." His face looked confused and she held up her hands in surrender. "I know, I know. I'm the one who started it. I never said it was rational."

Working together, they pulled the couch away from the wall and slid the loveseat back in its place. George caught her admiring his form and rolled his eyes. "Have a thing for moving men?"

"Maybe." She fanned herself to clinch the effect.

George finished moving the armchair and pulled her into it with him. He just held her, his chest rising and falling with the exertion of moving furniture. She rested her head in the crook of his neck, enjoying his cologne and the warmth of his skin.

Her phone chirped with a text message alert, and she shifted to pull it out of her back pocket. They bumped heads, both trying to read Martin's response at the same time.

I'll probably regret telling you this, but I am definitely not dating anyone else.

"Woohoo!" Emma hugged George. "It worked."

"And if that means Harriet moves away?"

Emma sighed. "If that's what makes her happy, then I guess I'll just find a new nurse."

He kissed her cheek. "I love you."

"I love you more."

His lips edged over to the soft spot behind her ear. "Is this a contest now?"

"I certainly hope so."

EPILOGUE ♥

"Introducing, Mr. and Mrs. Knightley!"

George gripped Emma's hand, and they made their grand entrance through the ballroom's double doors and out onto the dance floor. He wasn't a huge fan of being introduced by a D.J. amid strobe lights, but this was a once in a lifetime experience with the woman of his dreams. He'd hide his introverted nature for one night and take it all in. When the soulful strains of *At Last* by Etta James started up, he breathed a little easier and pulled Emma into his arms for their first dance while their photographer jogged around them, getting pictures from every angle.

Emma ran her thumbs along the back of his neck, tucking her head just under his chin. He instantly relaxed, loving the feel of her next to him.

"We did it, George," she whispered. "Tomorrow we'll be on a beach in Hawaii, toes in the sand…"

"Hiking through the jungle maybe?"

"Of course." She tilted her head up to kiss him, and he was happy to oblige.

One night, he'd told her about the little fantasy island he went to when he was stressed, and how it only added to his stress when she began appearing in it, wearing a tiny little sundress over a bikini, walking ahead of him on the trail. He'd never seen her laugh or blush so much in all the years he'd known her. When it was time to plan their honeymoon, they'd both agreed on Hawaii, and she'd blushed all over again.

147

Right now, she looked like an angel with her halo of white roses. He'd remember the scent of them and the look in her eyes forever. Waxing poetic again. That's what Emma would say if she could read his thoughts right now.

She was too good to him. A choreographed couple's dance was almost expected these days, but to him, that had sounded like two levels below Hades. Knowing him as well as she did, Emma had never even asked. They were probably boring their audience to death, but he was more than happy to sway back and forth with her in his arms.

His eyes swept the room, taking in John and Isabella, heads bent together, likely recalling their own first dance as a married couple. Little George was sitting on John's lap, his chubby face peering around and taking everything in. Betty, sitting next to them, patted Mr. Woodhouse's hand and whispered in his ear. He looked understandably nervous. The father-daughter dance was up next, and if anyone hated the spotlight more than George, it was that poor man.

Emma followed the direction of George's gaze. "He misses Harriet. She's good about calling him to chat, even when she's on the road with Martin. But Betty makes a wonderful nurse. I was afraid she'd have no interest after her mother died."

"Me too. I didn't think it would work out, but you were right to ask her. She fits right in with the rest of our crazy family."

"I tell Betty all the time, if she ever decides she needs to do something else, to just tell me. And she always responds with how I won't be rid of her that easily. I guess that means she likes her job." Emma looked up at him. "Everyone got their happily ever after."

"Thanks to your matchmaking," George said, softly touching his nose to hers.

Emma laughed. "Worst hobby ever."

"All's well that ends well, love." The song ended, and he twirled her out and gave her an elaborate bow, one he'd practiced as a little surprise.

Emma threw her arms around him. "Best day ever, George. Best day ever."

Thank you, lovely readers. Playing with Jane Austen's characters was a blast. Reviews are much appreciated. If you'd like to hear about new releases, you can follow my Amazon author page: www.amazon.com/author/racheljohn

Other titles by Rachel John:

Engaging Mr. Darcy
The Start of Us
Better With You
Anonymously Yours
Matchmaker for Hire
Bethany's New Reality
Not in the Plan
The Stand-in Christmas Date
The Truth About Running